PALADIN

A Pilgrimage Would Be Appropriate

Book 1

Middleman

Chapter One

—

Bloody Mercy

"Bones Picked Clean"
Ancaradis, Calyari
Third Day of the Month of Fire
34th Year of the reign of Patria Theodas Logos IV

The knife rested comfortably in the palm of my hand. It was a good piece of Trader steel, perfectly balanced. I considered throwing it. If it had Fate in the blade, it might do something impressive.

Deegan Grimes' three lackwits made a slow, predatory circle around me, snickering. Clotheslines full of linens dripped stinking indigo on our heads.

A dust dervish swept up a cloud of sand. Not far away, a liarbird spit out a stream of curses. On the other side of Cutpurse Bridge, merchants were hawking their wares. Over all that noise, my heartbeat still sounded like a drum in my ears.

Tussling with those young thugs was making me feel my age.

The leader of the three was a rich boy, about eighteen, quick, and sneaky. His boots said he came from money, but all the coin in the world wouldn't fix his nose. Rich Boy was a good fighter, and he'd already cut me once. Blood trickled from the wound. I ignored it. Back in my army days, I'd traded blows with people who actually intended to kill me.

Rich Boy squinted at the sun flashing off my Trader knife and swept in with a sloppy, overextended strike. I caught the top of his hand and pressed down between the bone and the gristle, bully-walking him into the wall. I slammed his back against the bricks and drove my knee into his gut. He puked and dropped his weapon, slurring some word I'd never heard before.

"Just off the boat from the Satrapies, eh?" I observed. "Nobody tell you to stay out of Bones Picked Clean?"

"Deegan..." The boy choked.

"Ooh, Deegan?" I kicked his knife into a pile of garbage. "You think I'm afraid of Deegan Grimes?"

My boys, watching from a nearby roof, cackled like a pack of hyenas.

"Ol' Leechface don't scare us!" Tig shouted. "I'd piss on his dead mother!"

"That's enough, Tig," I told him.

It was a mistake to get distracted. Seeing me turn my head, the dumbest and slowest of the thugs decided to swing at me again. He was easy pickings, and obviously didn't have the sense to stay down. I stepped to the left of his fist as he swung at me. Although I could've stabbed him, I put him on the ground instead. He dropped like he didn't have a bone in his body.

No surprise there. I've always favored my left.

I walked over to see if he was still conscious. When he looked up at me, I decided to make my feelings on him being in my District real clear.

"Deegan Grimes is a coward. He gets trash like you to

do his dirty work, cause he's afraid to cross Cutpurse Bridge," I said, crushing his hand with the heel of my boot. He shrieked and clawed at my ankle. "Now if you wanna keep your guts in your belly, you stay out of Bones Picked Clean! You got that?"

Something moved behind me, and I realized too late it was Rich Boy. I hadn't hurt him as bad as I'd thought, and I turned just in time for his fist to collide with my jaw.

There are some bad things about being real tall, and having a short man give you an uppercut is one of them. The whole world went fuzzy, but I managed not to get sucked down into the dark. When I staggered, Rich Boy jumped on my back like a monkey and tried to choke the air out of me.

I seized his belt and threw him over my shoulder like a sack of rice. Hucking rice sacks onto barges is the only legitimate work I've ever done, so it's fair to say I've got a certain skill for it. Without thinking, I put my blade between his ribs. The boy gasped. The blood that suddenly appeared on his lips told me I'd stabbed his lung. I hadn't meant to finish him off, but the poor idiot should've stopped when he was beat.

See... there's a reason folks call me Bloody Mercy.

As I stood up, I winced at a sharp pinch in my side and rubbed my jaw. I could feel the force of the punches I'd taken in my back teeth. The last of Deegan's boys saw the other two bleeding on the ground and decided he'd better run for it.

"You want us to go after him?" My boy Tig asked, looking down on me from above. Another of my boys, Lorne, was with him. They both crossed their arms and tried to look tough. Lorne is sixteen, with curly hair that makes him look like a girl, and he weighs maybe a hundred pounds soaking wet. Tig is even smaller, although older and meaner than his cousin.

They both jumped down to meet me, using the trash and the clotheslines to land like a couple of real professionals. Tig scratched his nose and spit a black glob of qaddi in the dust. I almost smacked him for picking up the nasty habit, but Lorne got him first.

"That shit rots your brains," Lorne said.

I nodded in agreement. "Makes your teeth fall out too."

Tig scowled. He didn't say anything back, but the look he gave me was easy to read. He was itching for a fight, and if I didn't give him something to do, he'd go find trouble.

"What are you waiting for, an invitation? If that fool can still run, he ain't hurtin' enough. Kick em' off the Bridge if you catch em'!"

Tig liked that idea. Him and Lorne both saluted and took off.

I muttered some choice words under my breath. Unless Deegan started keeping a tighter rein on his boys, I'd have to pay him a visit. The bastard was on the verge of starting another war between Deathwalker Alley and Bones Picked Clean.

As I was considering what to do next, I caught sight of a familiar figure turning the corner just ahead of me. I brushed myself off and sauntered over to meet the man, keeping my bloody hands behind my back.

My business partner Ferret raised an eyebrow in my direction.

"You've got blood on you, Mercy," he observed.

"Had to stab someone," I replied, keeping my voice low. We were being watched.

City guards in the Patria's colors of red and gold loitered on the street not far from Aerope's Apothecary. From the looks of things, it had been a bad day for them, and a bad day for Aerope too. The door to the little shop was torn off its hinges, and the air was filled with the sulfurous smell of arcane fire. Most of the tile roof was black. Shards of glass, piles of burned-up garbage, and nasty pools of caramelized potions were everywhere. Aerope was nowhere to be seen, and that made my stomach turn a loop.

Of course, the guards who'd been sent to handle the situation weren't helping clean up. They were "supervising" with their spears and blocking off the street.

"Don't be dumb, Mercy," Ferret warned, reading my face. He knew I wanted to say something about the guards interfering with the daily business of honest... well, folks I *liked*. Just like Deegan's boys, the Patria's toadies had no business mucking around in my territory.

"Suck an egg, Ferret," I told him, though I was going to follow his advice.

Fighting with city guards in Ancaradis is always a stupid thing to do. The Patria likes to keep his capital city heavily fortified, and for good reason. Calyari's northern neighbors, the kingdoms of Torres and Arborea, have been trying to wipe each other out for about five-hundred years.

The guards gave us the stink-eye. Even if they didn't know they were staring down the de-facto rulers of Bones Picked Clean, Ferret and I painted a strange picture standing in the only sliver of shade on the street.

I'm a good bit over six foot tall, pale as my Arborean

mother, and carrying a little extra weight around the middle. Every stitch of clothing I own was black once, but time has made it go gray. A bad scar from a wound that should've blinded me runs across the right side of my face. A fiend nearly tore my head off once. I like to tell that story when I'm drunk.

Ferret, my business partner, is Ksrali. How old he is, I don't know, but he's got some years on me. He doesn't have an ounce of meat anywhere on his bones, and the top of his head only reaches the middle of my chest. His skin is as dark as I've ever seen on a man, and his typical dress consists of a red and white striped kaftan that would look better on a woman. Ferret usually carries a huge patchwork bag that always seems to be filled with whatever he needs. Always perched on his shoulder is his pet liarbird, Cookie. Behind his thick glasses, his eyes are iridescent blue.

The Ksrali are an uncomfortable reminder that magic still lives in the south. Ferret's talents once made him the most notorious thief in Ancaradis. After losing a leg in an accident, he's since become the city's best fence.

With a flick of the wrist, Ferret passed me a pristine white handkerchief. Some patrician lady's initials were embroidered on it. I wiped sweat from my face. Cookie warbled, and Ferret fed him a piece of jerky. His thieving fingers were so quick that it looked like he pulled both the handkerchief and the jerky out of midair.

Maybe he did.

I was used to that sort of thing from him, so I just wiped my face clean. Still distracted by Aerope's mess, the guards didn't realize that someone had been murdered not forty feet away from them.

More likely, they didn't care.

Bones Picked Clean is the most dangerous slum in Ancaradis. The crimes that occur there never make it to court. We take care of our own trouble, and the folks who are found floating belly down in the Grand Canal have usually crossed certain lines. The fact that they're sent back to the Makers is something nobody mourns for long.

Ferret and I made our way back to the Dragon's Tail.

The Dragon's Tail is the worst public house in Bones Picked Clean, and that's saying something. The District doesn't have any businesses apart from public houses, and the occasional "don't ask, don't tell" apothecary like Aerope.

The walls of the Tail are made of earth covered in whitewash, and they stink when it rains. Kegs serve as tables, shipping crates are chairs, and a mound of musty pillows fills the corner where the qaddi chewers sleep. Watered-down beer, burnt bread, and cheap, nasty meat are the only things on the menu. Of course, the regulars don't come in because they're hungry.

In short, the Dragon's Tail is where people go if they want to buy anything, sell anything, steal anything... or have someone killed.

I should know. I own the place.

When the two of us good businessmen walked into our fine establishment, the common room was as sparse as it usually was before the sun went down. One of our regulars, an old qaddi addict called "No Teeth" was absorbed in a dice game with the bartender, bouncer, and cook.

Incidentally, all that's just one man.

The Tail's only employee is a burly Northman with a name everybody chokes on, so we call him "Guts". Most of the time, he doesn't seem to be working... but to be fair, he rarely gets paid. Like most people who hang around the Tail, he doesn't have anywhere else to go.

Another regular, a half-Trader drunkard known as "Windrider", was passed out in the corner of the room when Ferret and I arrived. A pair of Trader women were sitting with her, sucking on a hookah and sharpening their long knives. The Traders gave me nasty catlike smiles as I walked past them. Their bells and bracelets made a lot of noise as they worked their blades. Some say that the Trader's characteristic jingling is a warning, like the rattle of a venomous snake.

I noticed that one of the two Traders had silver spirals on her face and walked a little quicker. Traders like to cause trouble, and because of an ancient bargain, they're literally immune to the Laws of Men. Their Fatecrafters, with the spooky tattooed faces, are the worst.

Now, what us Calyareans call "the Laws of Men", a foreigner would call "Fate". Most folks can't escape what Fate has in store for them, but Traders craft their destinies like a smith crafts metal. Some of them can give a piece of bread to a rat and through a series of unrelated coincidences cause a bridge to collapse. Legally, any mess caused by a Fatecrafter falls under the jurisdiction "Acts of the Gods" along with fires, hurricanes, and floods. It's a fairly potent reminder that while most Traders look normal enough, they're not exactly human.

As I approached the bar, the distinctive smell of Trader's

Fire caught my attention. Although they're chiefly known for fatemangling and their horses, Traders also brew the meanest hooch known to man. It will kill whatever ails you, and give you a fleeting touch of Sight. Like most people born and raised in the slums, I'd been addicted to the shit most of my life.

Guts poured me a good amount of Trader's Fire from a dark green bottle. I examined the amber-colored liquor. It smelled like honey and red pepper, and I could already tell it was going to be strong. I drank it down. The burn was perfect.

I slammed my glass on the bar. "Damn! That hits the spot! Get me another."

"They sell," Guts said, gesturing to the Traders.

"Good. Buy as much as they've got," I replied.

Guts wrinkled his nose and poured me a double. He didn't share my affection for Trader's Fire, but he was also afraid of turmeric and garlic. Sometimes it amazed me that he'd survived in Calyari for as long as he had.

I drained my second glass of Trader's Fire and was getting a hot coal for the hookah when a girl blazed through my front door. She was wearing a bad yellow wig and dressed in a flimsy white nightgown, which made it obvious that her body was mostly bones rather than womanly curves. All the tin jewelry in the world wouldn't make her look like a foreign beauty. She was a local girl, and in my opinion, too young to be whoring. The name she usually went by was "Snow".

I doubted she'd ever seen snow. I had, and I didn't think it was pretty or romantic. Mostly, it was just cold.

"Mercy!" Snow shouted.

"I'm right here, girl," I said.

Snow jumped, realizing I was near enough to bite her. I knew she was afraid of me, but I didn't think much of it. Most sensible people are afraid of me.

"Some of Deegan's men have come into the Pearl, and they won't leave!" Snow hissed. She clearly meant to whisper, but she spoke awfully loud regardless. "Big Alice sent me to get you."

"*Again*?" I groaned.

Snow nodded. Ferret rolled his eyes.

"Guts? Give me my sword," I ordered.

Guts tossed me what I'd asked for, the sword that usually rusted on the wall above the fireplace. It was army issue, an ugly, badly-balanced piece of junk, but I'd spent more than half my life wielding it. Now, running around with a weapon in Ancardis is a good way to get arrested, unless you're a Guild mercenary or one of the Patria's men. It wasn't my habit to go out with a sword on my hip, but I knew Deegan Grimes liked to play at being a patrician and always carried a blade when he was out making trouble.

Ferret's liarbird landed on my head. "Don't be dumb, Mercy," Cookie croaked. "Dumb Mercy!"

"Does that buzzard of yours ever say anything else?" I demanded, shooing him off.

Ferret only shrugged.

"Over an' over," No Teeth said. It was the first garbled thing that had come out of his mouth since I'd arrived, not that I was surprised. He was a longtime qaddi addict, and his brains rarely worked. "Got to say it over an' over," he added.

I didn't bother to correct No Teeth, but I had a lot of

experience with fiends. Liarbirds didn't need to be trained like parrots. They could talk like men if they had the mind to, and they understood *everything* they heard.

When Cookie returned to Ferret, I looked straight into the creature's beady eyes. "Dumb Mercy likes to eat turkey," I warned him. "And you're fat enough to pass for one, you filthy flying rat!"

The liarbird squawked defiantly and fluttered off, landing on the head of the Fatecrafter. She reached up to scratch the mangy fiend with a little smile on her face. I did not like that smile in the least. I wasn't a god-fearing man, but having a Fatecrafter smirk at me almost sent me running for the nearest temple.

Then I remembered I had business to take care of.

"All right. Let's go save Alice," I said, herding Snow out the back door of the Tail. She almost tripped over the hem of her nightgown, and I noticed that she didn't have shoes on. Obviously, she'd left the Pearl in a hurry, which meant that the situation was already bad... and probably getting worse.

The last thing I heard clearly as we headed in the direction of Cutpurse Bridge was Windrider waking up from her alcohol-induced nap. "Damnit, Guts!" She groaned.

Sure enough, when I took a good whiff, I could smell bread burning. Snow raised an eyebrow in my direction.

Even with the meanest man in Ancaradis right behind her, she still looked nervous. "I tell ya, sweetheart," I sighed heavily. "Good help is hard to find."

Chapter Two

—

Friends in Low Places

Red Lantern District
Ancaradis, Calyari
Third Day of the Month of Fire

The Pearl of the East sits on the border of Bones Picked Clean and Deathwalker Alley, which makes the whorehouse a point of contention between Deegan Grimes and myself. It used to be that Deegan had the place when Big Alice was still his woman, but after I killed the former owner of the Dragon's Tail, the old girl and I had sorted out our differences and came to an arrangement which suited us both.

If I kept her "sweeties" from getting harassed by Deegan's lowlives, my boys got a solid discount, and I got a good source of information. The part where Big Alice and I fell into bed together wasn't planned, but I considered it a nice bonus. Deegan saw it as the worst betrayal imaginable, and he set out to get revenge on Big Alice with the same kind of malice he'd formerly reserved for me.

Now, Big Alice is the most famous good-time girl in Ancaradis. The Pearl is the nicest house in the slums, and Alice knows how to throw parties that get talked about even up on Oleander Hill.

The two of us are alike in that we both get mistaken for

foreigners, although we were raised Calyarean. Alice's father was an Arborean mercenary, driven south by the same war that brought my mother to Ancaradis. Not counting her looks, Alice is Calyarean through and through. She dresses like she's one of the Patria's daughters, always decked out in pearls and waltzing around with a floofy ostrich feather fan. She can cook, out-drink any man, and throw most scumbags right out the doors of her own brothel. In addition to being a born tussler, there's lots of her to go around, which is something I appreciate. Her curves could cause a dead man to check his pulse, and she screams like a banshee when she's having a good time.

If I was the marrying type, I'd maybe propose to her. Just imagining how Deegan would hate the two of us living together brought a smile to my face. Still, I knew better than to underestimate the old bastard. He had more boys than I did, and he didn't hesitate to gamble with their lives like they were fighting roosters. I had to outfox him.

Instead of going in the front door of the Pearl, I slipped through the courtyard around back where the girls did their washing. Climbing up the trellis on the side of the building all the way up to the third floor, I craned my neck to see what I could of the situation. Though I'm not particularly agile, I've been in and out of Big Alice's window a few times.

I had one leg over the balcony railing when both Big Alice and Deegan noticed that I was trying to sneak up on them. Deegan snarled and threw open the doors.

Now, when I say "threw", I mean Deegan took those doors clean off their hinges. When Deathwalkers are angry or surprised, the fiend in them seizes control. Deegan moved like an animal, and he looked like one too. Although he likes shiny baubles and flashy clothes, he's always filthy, which is how you can tell he's not a real patrician. Patricians love their fancy baths and some of them go almost every day. I've never been in one of those places myself, but I've heard tell they're worth the expense.

"Mercy!" Deegan sneered.

"Mercy!" Big Alice tried to grab Deegan, but one of his boys caught her by the hair. She seized a gilded candlestick from the mantel of her fireplace, and laid him out with a blow to the head. I grimaced, knowing from experience that her fancy little decoration was made of solid pig iron.

I didn't have time to worry about Big Alice with Deegan coming right for me. The toe of my boot was stuck in the trellis, and I furiously tried to shake my foot free. Without hesitation, Deegan clocked me good in the face, and I tasted copper. I drew my sword and lunged at him, although my trapped foot kept me off-balance. He stabbed back at me but got only cloth, putting yet another hole in the shoulder of my ragged shirt. Of course, that was when the piece of wood that kept the trellis attached to the side of the Pearl decided that it had suffered enough.

I heard somebody, probably Big Alice, shout my name as the trellis tore free from the brick and pitched backwards into the canal.

Now, falling into a canal anywhere in Ancaradis is bad, but on the border of Deathwalker Alley it can be fatal. People throw all kinds of things they need to get rid of into the canals, and the nastier the neighborhood, the nastier the stuff.

My first love had been a clever little thief from Dyer's Row. One day, she disappeared. My mother told me that she'd gone to live with relatives in the country. I discovered years later that she'd actually fallen into a canal and impaled herself on the remains of a ballista. As I sank into the water, I realized I couldn't remember that poor girl's name.

Pieces of Big Alice's balcony were floating all around me, but the bricks stuck to the trellis were making it sink. I heard a hollow thunk as the trellis struck the bottom of the canal, and for a moment I stared into the grinning maw of a tied-up corpse.

I fumbled with my boot, tweaking my foot as I yanked it out. There was no breath left in me when I made it to the surface. I gasped for air, and a crossbow bolt zipped over my shoulder. Despite the stench of piss and lamp oil, I dove back into the water. I couldn't see where my sword had gone, or lay my hands on anything that might be a weapon.

When I had to go up for air again, Deegan and his boys were busting through the kitchen of the Pearl. I was surrounded before I heaved myself out of the canal, weaponless, and short one boot.

I held my hands up in a gesture of surrender. While crossbows don't reload quickly, they're powerful enough to punch through armor, and I wasn't even wearing my good shirt.

Deegan slowly approached me. He made it look like laziness, but I knew it was fear that kept him out of my reach. When he was close enough to get a good whiff of the canal, he grimaced and coughed into his sleeve. Apparently the stench was enough to make anyone gag, even a Deathwalker.

"Jack Mercy," Deegan observed. "Even more *disgusting* than usual."

"You're wasting your breath, Deathwalker," I retorted. "All the soap in the world wouldn't scrub the shit out of you. Nice pigsticker though," I observed Deegan's sword. Hard not to, as he had it pointed at my throat. It was a gaudy piece of work, and I hadn't seen it before. I guessed it was a recent acquisition, and I was mentally sorting out the best way to take it away from him.

"Hasn't tasted a drop of blood yet," Deegan said, sounding smug.

"You want to test it out on me? Call off your boys and we'll have ourselves a proper duel, like a couple of fancy-pants patricians." Of course, I knew Deegan wouldn't take my offer. In a fair fight, I'd win, but even if he got lucky and killed me, he'd be in a world of trouble.

My boys would finish off most of Deegan's gang to avenge my death, and lots of folks who didn't work for either of us would quickly take sides. Deegan would have to fight off Cutpurse Bridge, the Docks, Red Lantern and maybe even Lighthouse Hill. A lot of people would get stabbed, and nobody would make any money for months. At least, it had been that way when Old Man Percy, the most senior man in the slums, had gotten rid his predecessor.

"Perish the thought. You look like a drowned rat, and you haven't got a weapon. When I take your life, and note that I did say 'when', we will be evenly matched. There's no honor in besting a man at a disadvantage," Deegan replied.

Deegan treating me like I was scum was nothing new. I didn't consider it much of an insult, coming from a man who had a fiend living in his brains, and eating him from the inside. While I couldn't find the words to insult him back, I did notice that he hadn't said anything about me killing one of his new recruits.

Was Rich Boy dead? Did Deegan know? Did he care? None of those questions sat well with me.

I watched the crossbows, and kept my mouth shut.

"Pathetic," Deegan sneered. "Leave him."

His boys relaxed just a little, and started to back away. The smart thing would've been to count myself lucky and let them go.

But me, I'm dumb.

I saw the last of Deegan's boys hesitate, and that felt like an opening.

"Come along," Deegan said, looking right at the boy. The poor idiot turned his back on me, and I let him take just two steps before I put my new Trader knife to his throat and made sure he felt the steel. The boy, properly spooked, let out an "oof" and immediately dropped his crossbow.

If Deegan hadn't known me as well as he did, he might have accused me of being a Trader and crafting Fate to my advantage. The rest of the boys whirled around and their crossbows came right back up. Of course, where I stood, not one of them could get a clear shot at me, especially not while I was using one of their own as a shield.

"Put down your weapons," I ordered.   "You too, Deathwalker."

Deegan narrowed his eyes. He drew his sword.

"You can't fight us all," he said.

"I don't have to fight any of you," I replied. "Not if you want your boy back in one piece. You know I don't bluff, old man. Consider it a tax for harassing Alice."

Deegan hesitated. I wasn't sure if he was going to charge me or drop his blade and back off like I'd asked him to. I don't like killing folk, but I'm real good at giving the impression that I'll gut just about anyone.

I felt pretty smart right then, but that feeling was short-lived.

"Mercy!" One of Big Alice's girls shouted from a second-floor window. "Soldiers are coming!"

The clank of armor got my attention right away. Stomping down the middle of the road were a dozen legionnaires. Unlike the city guards who were usually young patricians putting in an easy two years of military service, legionnaires weren't inclined to ignore lawbreaking just because they might get a little blood on their tabards.

I didn't want to tangle with real soldiers, and neither did Deegan.

"Looks like it's your lucky day, leechface," I said, using my boy Tig's name for the old bastard.

"This isn't over, Mercy!" Deegan warned. Though normally he wouldn't have left without issuing a few more puffed-up threats, Deegan was tainted. If the legionnaires caught him, he wasn't going to spend a few months locked up on a barge or breaking rocks in a prison camp. While I'd never seen Deegan raise fiends like a real Deathwalker, the scelera of his eyes had gone black years ago. As the Patria saw it, that was evidence enough to execute him for practicing magic.

I ran in the back door of the Pearl, and two of Big Alice's girls shoved me into the pantry. While Big Alice put on a performance for her guests, I shook a biting crab out of my remaining boot and looked for something I could clobber someone with. I settled on a broom. Fortunately, I didn't have to test my weapon against the Patria's steel. When the door to the pantry opened, it was Big Alice who got a face full of dusty straw. I saw who she was just in time to pull my blow. Big Alice coughed, and slapped me hard with her open hand. Then she grimaced, realizing she'd gotten canal slime on her fingers.

She blinked in surprise as she saw the biting crab scuttling across the floor. "Gods! Yuck!" Big Alice seized the broom from me and whacked the crab until it stopped moving. "Oh, Mercy! What am I going to do with you? With all these little fiends you've drug into my pantry, I'm going to need the Order of Light to perform an exorcism!"

"The Order of Light?" I echoed. That was something I hadn't heard mentioned in a long while.

"You haven't heard?" Big Alice laughed at the expression on my face. "Word is, there are wizards in town."

"Hunh," I paused. "Is that what the legionnaires are after?"

Magic was against the law in Calyari, but despite the Patria's decree, the slums were always rife with witches, fortune-tellers, and Deathwalkers like Deegan who'd speak with the dead or arrange murders for a price. Wizards were much more powerful than the usual magic-wielding miscreants, and they carried the protection of the King of Torres. Technically, a wizard setting foot in Calyari was a breach of the treaty that had ended the last war. But if wizards from the Order of Light *had* come to Ancaradis, that explained why Aerope's shop was currently in ruins. Wizards spent a whole lot of their time hunting down Deathwalkers. It was like cats and rats with them.

"Did you think they were looking for *you*?" Big Alice put her hands on her hips.

"I was *hoping* they were looking for Deegan," I replied.

"Dana's tits, I only wish!" Big Alice rolled her eyes. "There's going to be trouble soon, Mercy," she informed me, as if that was something I couldn't guess.

"I'll protect you," I promised. "Don't I always?"

Big Alice leaned in and kissed me very quickly. "Thank you," she whispered.

"All you have to do is ask," I replied. The kiss didn't last as long as I would have liked. Although being soaked to the bone with canal water made me want to retch, Big Alice smelled like jasmine and sandalwood. I pulled her closer.

"Oh no! You're not getting anything else until *you* take a bath!" She laughed, shoving me out the door.

Chapter Three

—

A Mysterious Message

"Bones Picked Clean"
Ancaradis, Calyari
Third Day of the Month of Fire

I made my way back to the Tail, running as fast as I could with no boots on. I needed to lie low, though not because of Deegan Grimes. If wizards had already found Aerope, I might be next on their list. It was common knowledge that I'd once been in the service of Idun Raima, the infamous Deathwalker who'd nearly conquered Calyari. Even amongst thieves and thugs, there are some confessions which make folks raise their eyebrows, and admitting you once worked for "Fiend Raima" is one of those.

Usually, I reminded people that I'd signed on with the fiend when my other option was "death". While that was true, Lord Raima had treated me better than the Patria's army.

I'd been seventeen when the war started, old enough to be conscripted, but still young enough to believe that legionnaires led a good life. After six years, I received my first month of paid leave. I got wise, ditched the army, and signed on with a mercenary company instead. Being a merc suited me, and I stayed with the Guild up until the massacre at the Vermilion River. That battle broke me. I thought I'd never experience anything worse.

There was a lot I didn't know in those days.

See, working for Deathwalkers is dangerous business. Apart from the black magic, the fiends, and the numerous enemies... there's always the possibility that sooner or later, your master will decide you'd be more interesting if your soul was trapped in the corpse of a dog and your spine was made into a piece of furniture. Fortunately for me, Lord Raima appreciated the fact that I was mostly obedient, and not easy to kill. I resisted his attempts to break my will.

Resisting his daughter Aerope wasn't so easy. She and I became lovers, and with her insistence, I was promoted from her father's "dog" to his "Left Hand". I had the best of anything we could get our claws on, and complete authority over the other mercs, slaves, and garden-variety lunatics in Lord Raima's service. The only thing I didn't control was the fiends. I wasn't sorry for that. The black magic was the only thing I never could stomach, even when I saw how useful it was. Still, if we'd had any chance of winning, I would've stuck with House Raima until the end. Sure, they were Deathwalkers, but at least they were honest about that, and in my experience, a bad man who pretended to be a good man was more dangerous than a bad man who just knew what he was.

An uneasy alliance with Torres kept the Patria's army from falling apart, and then things started looking not too good for us. The wizards of the Order of Light finished off my former master, and I escaped by the skin of my teeth. Aerope came with me. For about two years, things were as good as I'd ever hoped they could be, but then Aerope started losing control of her inner fiend.

After the second time she tried to kill me, I left her my at mother's house and moved into a small room above the Dragon's Tail. Bones Picked Clean wasn't a very big District, so I couldn't ignore her, but when we passed one another on the street, I stayed on the left side, and Aerope stayed on the right. In a way, it was as if her father was still between us.

Windrider and No Teeth were having a smoke at the Tail when I got home. The sun was beginning to go down, and I was relieved to see that the Traders were gone. While Guts heated some water for my much-needed bath, I sat down and rubbed my sore feet. I was pissed that I'd lost both my sword and my boots in one day, and I was worried about Aerope. I also couldn't forget what Big Alice had said about wizards.

Now, Windrider is nominally part of my gang, but I trust her somewhat less than Deegan Grimes. She's not a real Trader, a halfblood at best, but odd and irritating things still happen around her. She also has the bad habit of not paying for her booze.

Windrider passed me the hookah, probably because I looked like I needed it. I took a long draw and sighed in relief. Cookie picked something out of my hair that I suspected was more carrion from the canal. I didn't bother to curse or swing at the liarbird. All things considered, I'd rather have a fiend perched on my shoulder than insects crawling around in my hair.

"My cousin wanted me to give you a message," Windrider said. I figured she was talking about the Traders. Although she never left Ancaradis, she liked to sound like she was fresh out of the desert. Mostly, she came off like a Calyarean pretending to be a Trader, but I didn't tell her so. "You must seek your father."

"My father?" I echoed incredulously. I'd never known my father, and Windrider was well-aware of that. "Is your cousin chewing qaddi?"

Windrider turned her nose up at me, but I figured that was because I'd implied that her prophesy spewing "cousin" was consuming crud known to cause hallucinations. "Meretry is *ja Mazrin*," she said. *Mazrin* was the Trader word for "Fatecrafter".

I twitched slightly, remembering the woman with the tattooed face. Though all Traders were slippery, Fatecrafters were the worst. They could make anyone do anything, and there was no way of dodging their plans. A fatemangle could start with something as simple as stepping on a cockroach.

"Well, you tell your cousin that I don't want her help, you got that? I do just fine on my own," I paused. "Where's Ferret?" I asked.

Cookie yanked on my hair. A fat black water beetle landed belly-up on the table, and the liarbird greedily swallowed it down.

"Disgusting," Windrider wrinkled her nose.

"Sure is," I agreed. "Guts is drawing me a bath right now."

"You sure about that?" Windrider asked.

I felt hot water on the floor, flowing under my feet.

"Damnit!" I cursed. "Guts!" I shouted.

The kitchen door flew open, and it was Ferret who stormed out. The sound of him coming or going is unmistakable. Having only one leg, he still hurries everywhere, and whacks anything that gets in his way with his crutch.

Ferret thumped his way over to the bar, and noticed a black crust of bread sitting there. He seized it and pitched it into the kitchen as hard as he could. It hit something with a metallic thunk. A crash followed.

"What's gotten into you, Ferret? Why's there water everywhere?" I was getting real unhappy with the circumstances, so I rose to my feet to make a point.

"*Dabi! Pak naayata!*" A familiar voice shouted from the kitchen.

"*Raaku oma!*" Ferret hit the door with his crutch. It swung hard the other direction, and the knob knocked a chunk of plaster out of the wall.

I sat right back down.

Swinging a cast-iron skillet like a mace and spitting curses, Coriander came flying out of the kitchen, like the door wasn't even in her way. Ferret held up his crutch like a shield. He blocked the woman attacking him, but only barely.

"Ooof. You're not going to break them up?" Windrider observed.

"Nope," I replied, drawing on the hookah again. "The missus is *crazy*."

Ferret's wife Coriander made up for being even smaller than he was with her big voice and even bigger attitude. She normally worked the street around the Offices of Commerce and was as good of a grifter as Ferret was a thief. Whatever the two were having it out about, they were doing it in loud, fast, Ksrali which I couldn't follow.

Guts stood with his arms crossed in the kitchen door. He cleared his throat, which sounded like a man being killed, and motioned for Coriander to give him his skillet. The Northman is even bigger than I am. Ferret and Coriander looked like children in his shadow.

"*Fakhali!*" Coriander snapped, pointing at Ferret with a scowl on her face. That word translated as "lazy house-dweller" and it's a pretty fierce insult in Ksrali. Ferret sighed, looking subdued.

"*Nana, bhit mayu!*" He protested. Those were also words I knew. What they mean, as I understood it, is "I don't understand the problem!" It's Ferret's way of ending most arguments with his wife.

"*Heeka,*" Coriander snorted, dismissing him. She slammed her skillet down on the bar and poured herself a mug full of Trader's Fire, which she downed like it was nothing at all. I waited until she'd cooled down some, and then I came to sit next to her. Realizing I wasn't going to be getting my bath right away, I poured myself a bit of the brew.

"Trouble with the mister?" I asked.

Coriander gave me a look of death, and I knew I was about to get an earful. "I lost five dina today, and it's all his fault! There were two lovely little Patricians playing the tables at Percy's this morning, and I would have had them *both* if Feret hadn't interrupted me to tell me about some stupid damned fire! Why should I care what happens to Aerope? She's mad as a dragon, and sooner or later, *someone* was going to put her down! Weylan's Teeth, this District has gone to pot!"

"You've been saying that for ten years," I reminded her, pouring her some more Trader's Fire. Because Ferret was my business partner, we'd agreed that his wife didn't have to pay for her drinks at the Tail. It was a concession that I usually regretted making, but slighting Coriander was dangerous. She wasn't very strong, but she fought dirty and would use anything she could get her hands on as a weapon.

"It's been true for ten years," Coriander sighed. "I assume you know what happened?"

"Assume I don't," I said. Since sunup, I'd done nothing but get into fights. I'd seen what Aerope's Apothecary looked like, but nobody had told me how it got to be that way. Both the guards and the legionnaires were out in force, and I recalled that Alice had said something about *wizards*.

"The Patria's men arrested Aerope this morning," Coriander explained. "Tomorrow they'll cut her head off."

"So?" It was a natural progression for Deathwalkers. I'd always known that the magic Aerope wielded would send her kicking and screaming into the dark. When she'd first followed me to Ancaradis, I'd scrounged every coin I could so that she could undergo frequent purifications, and have the most effective fiend-sealing brandings. Eventually, the pain became too much for her, and she stopped praying at the Temple. I realized that she was drifting towards the darkness again when she started acting like her father.

"You loved her once," Coriander reminded me.

I snorted, pretending I didn't care.

Coriander gave me a silly, smug look. Years after Aerope and I had gone our separate ways, I still let her live in my mother's house. I still sent desperate people to her business, and chased off the priests and soldiers who might hassle her. If Aerope was about to be executed, I did owe her a farewell. She'd have a hard time killing me from inside a prison cell. I could say my piece, and maybe if there was anything still human in her, that part would hear it.

I scrubbed myself clean of the canal first, not that I figured a fiend would care if I had beetles in my hair. I also strapped on a few knives. Citizens weren't technically permitted on the docks, but a little coin would grease the palms of one of the guards I owned. He'd let me in to see Aerope, whom I assumed would be off limits to visitors.

To say that Ancaradis has "a problem with crime" is like saying the ocean has "a problem with fish". For as long as I've been alive, the Patria's prison has been overflowing. After the last war, anyone caught for petty crime more than three times was put "on ship" and sent up to the Satrapies. The punishments for using or abusing magic became especially severe. An old tobacco warehouse on the west side of the harbor was converted into a cell block, and the huge flat stone that had formerly served as the resting place of the Patria's pleasure boat, became the site of the hardest-working gallows in all of Calyari.

Though most thieves and thugs won't be caught anywhere near the Docks because the Patria's men are everywhere, there's a big difference between being a common cutpurse and the de-facto ruler of a District. My bought guard gave me an odd look when I asked where Aerope was, but he didn't ask my business.

I found Aerope sleeping in a cell on a brig ironically called *"Bright Future"*. When I saw her, I had to steady myself. I'd severely underestimated my weakness for that woman. I couldn't remember the last time I'd laid eyes on her, but she hadn't aged a day. She'd always been beautiful, with an olive complexion and long, curly black hair. Born into a patrician family, Aerope couldn't have been more different than Big Alice, tall and thin with graceful hands and a nose that made her look exactly like the ancient statue of Ilshanna the Sorceress that I'd seen out in the desert on my first long march with the army.

Part of me wanted to wake Aerope, to break her free, and make a run for it. With her magic and my fighting skills, it would take a lot to bring us down. Then I reminded myself of the last time the two of us had been alone together. Despite how she looked, Aerope was not the woman I'd fallen in love with. The fiend had won. I forced myself to stare at the black brands on her neck and hands. They reminded me that I'd lost the real Aerope a long time ago, and I was not in a hurry to sacrifice myself to a fiend's insatiable hunger.

Aerope yawned and sat up. She turned to face me in a sharp, twitchy manner, like a marionette puppet whose strings were being pulled. A cold chill raced down my spine as I remember Lord Raima waking up exactly like that. What I was looking at was not a living woman at all, but a soulless corpse animated by a fiend as smart as a man. Aerope noticed where I waited and opened her eyes. They were a pure, solid black.

"Hello, Jack," she smiled sweetly. I flinched slightly, though I didn't want to show any weakness. Tendrils of shadow, almost invisible to the naked eye, danced around her. Though she couldn't use any devastating magic while bound with blessed shackles, I could still feel her trying to dig her claws into my mind.

"Long time no see, Aerope," I replied. "How long has it

been? Two years? Three?"

"Jack, I'm still living in your mother's house," She reminded me. "I know your people spy on me. You could come to see me at any time."

"And why should I? You tried to kill me!" I demanded.

"Pff! If I'd tried to kill you, you'd be dead! And if you would just listen, I wouldn't have to hurt you at all," She said all that with a casual toss of her curls, like trying to murder me didn't mean much of anything.

"Listen my ass! You only play innocent when you want something," I informed her. "And I'm only here because you're going to be executed," I paused. "*I told you so.*"

"Liar!" Aerope sighed heavily, her hands on her hips. "You're rescuing me, aren't you?"

"No," I replied. "Not this time. You keep doing this. You put yourself here. This time you can get yourself out. And maybe think about what you've been doing."

"Feh! You're no saint yourself, Jack!" Aerope reminded me. "It could just as easily be you in this cell!"

"No, we are not the same," I snapped. "I bust noses and break fingers! You turn folks inside out and suck their souls out of them. That is *not* the same! I'm not saying I'm a good man, damnit, but there are lines you don't cross. And you ought to know that better than anyone! Do you want to be your father? Do you? Cause that's what it looks like to me!"

Aerope wrinkled her nose. "So, I suppose you're here to lecture me about how *me* killing for my needs is wrong, while *you* killing for two lousy streets in a slum is business?"

"Dana's tits, I can't talk to you when you're like this! How long has your fiend been running you this time? Two weeks? Three?" I pressed. The way she looked at me I knew

I'd guessed right. "You know what the difference between us is? I do what people force me to! You do *whatever you want!*"

"Ooh, I hate when you're like this! Has it never occurred to you that maybe you do what you want to, and you only convince yourself that you're being forced to do it?" A very strange look came over her face, and I realized slowly that she was still, at least partially, under the fiend's control. *"You're just like your father."*

I remembered what Windrider had told me earlier, and felt the blood freeze in my veins. Aerope had never met my father... or at least, the human Aerope hadn't. Maybe I'd been talking to the fiend all along?

"What do you know about my father, fiend?" I demanded, grabbing the bars of the cell as if I intended to tear them right out of the wall. That turned out to be a mistake. Faster than I could see, the creature that used to be Aerope seized my hands and dug her nails into the undersides of my wrists, drawing blood like a sharp razor. I tore away from her and staggered backwards into the guards that had come running.

Aerope's shape became fluid, and tendrils of black miasma struck the bars of her cell like a dozen bullwhips. The ship lurched, and the guards all stared in horror at the fiend behind me. There was a priest with them. He didn't panic, just put his hands together, bowed his head, and whispered a prayer.

The fiend hissed like a snake as the blessing on her shackles triggered, flaring with white-gold light and making a ringing sound like a temple bell. I hadn't been so close to white magic in a long time. I'd almost forgotten how damned disorienting it was. Unlike black magic, which tends to be slimy and insidious, white magic is kinda like getting hit in the face with a huge, shiny brick.

I didn't explain myself and shoved my way out the door, diving over the railing of the ship when someone yelled at me to stop. I swam as far as Cutpurse Bridge with torches and lanterns following me the whole way. A fight outside a brothel drew the attention of the Patria's men just long enough for me to climb out of the canal and slip in the back door of Percy's.

Coriander saw me standing there in the shadows looking like a drowned rat, and left her usual table. We went into the kitchen, and she helped me clean out my wounds while the cook cut me some bandages. As talkative as she usually was, Ferret's little wife didn't say anything. She obviously felt sorry for me, and I didn't try to tell her that I was okay. Though I knew better than to put stock in the words of a fiend, I worried that Aerope was right, and that I *was* about to get what I deserved.

Of course, that wasn't the worst of it. After hearing both Windrider and Aerope's fiend mention my father, my mind was inventing all kinds of Fates that I didn't like at all, mostly involving Traders, white wizards, and especially my former lover.

You see, when dealing with Deathwalkers, it's not dying that's scary.

It's *not* dying.

Chapter Four

—

Fiend Raima

North of the Vermilion River
The Sea of Sands, Calyari
24th Year of the reign of Patria Theodas Logos IV

Ten Years Ago

A bitter, cold wind blew sand in my eyes. I squinted. The night sky was filled with stars, a ribbon of gauzy white that seemed to float from one end of the heavens to the other. I'd always heard it called "Dana's Veil", although according to the Traders it was a river of milk produced by the god Yfaar's celestial mares. Those stars usually couldn't be seen, except on the coldest winter nights. They seemed so pure and clean, especially in comparison to the scorched, bloody ground all around me.

I realized that I was dreaming when I looked down at my hands.

I was dressed in good armor, the kind that I hadn't owned in years. My tabard was red and blue, the unmistakable colors of the Mercenary's Guild. If the smells I remembered were any indication, I was somewhere out in the godforsaken Sea of Sands. There was a blue shield lying on the ground next to me, with the device of a white fox holding a broken arrow in its mouth.

Madelin's Raiders.

The last time I'd seen that heraldry was on a night I'd never forgotten. Knowing I was dreaming didn't make me feel better. I took a deep breath, trying to steady myself. My nerves were raw, and my body ached. Exhaustion had seeped into my soul, and I didn't give a damn about anything. Nothing mattered.

I was about to die.

The soldier behind me forced me to my knees. He didn't say a word, but he kept his hand firmly planted on my shoulder. Clearly, I was supposed to stay down. I stared at the ground, at least until the soldier cuffed me across the back of the head with his steel gauntlet. "Sonova bitch!" I cursed, glaring at him. "What was that for?"

The soldier didn't answer me. Then again, I had no reason to believe that he was capable of actual speech. The stories I'd heard about Fiend Raima's minions seemed to suggest that half of them were dead men, and the rest had never been men at all.

I counted the soldiers. There were at least twenty surrounding us, not including the one behind me. My Guild Brother, Mio, was lying flat on his face with another of the fiend's minions standing on his back. He looked terrified, but he was only eighteen. He'd been with the Guild not even six months, and he wasn't formerly sworn in. Madelin wouldn't have considered him a full member of her Company, but she was dead, and the rest of us were trying to carry on without her. For the most part, that meant rushing new recruits out to the battlefield long before they were ready.

My Guild Sister, Cecily, the only other survivor of the original Raiders, wasn't being restrained, but that didn't matter. She'd been bleeding from a gut wound for three days, since the Vermilion River. Mio and I had carried her across the desert, hoping to make it as far as Chalceda. From the way she was breathing, I felt sure that her life was ebbing away. I found myself hoping that Cecily would go quick. Though I hated to lose her, there were fates worse than death, and we were currently facing one of them.

The leader of the fiends slowly approached me. He walked like an arrogant patrician, and there were spurs on the heels of his tall black boots. His face was concealed by a silver mask, and his helm was an old Western style, probably a family heirloom. A mantle of very fine riveted chain hung over his shoulders. He had an elegant sword, and a dagger tucked into a sash around his waist. He wore that dagger like a Trader long knife, and from the way he stood, I suspected he could draw it and cut my throat faster than I could punch him in the gut. There was a silver lotus on the weapon's pommel, the insignia of House Raima.

The masked man who'd been pursuing us since the Vermilion River wasn't just another of the fiend's faceless minions. He was someone with clout. We'd been hunted down for a reason.

"A most impressive chase," the masked man remarked.

"Piss off," I told him. The soldier behind me hit me with his gauntlet again. "If you hit me with that thing one more time, I'm going to beat you to death with it!" I snapped.

"They're going to *kill* us, Mercy," Mio said.

"All the more reason not to cooperate," I retorted.

The masked man laughed slightly, observing our Guild pins.

"Who do you serve, mercenary?" He asked me.

"I don't think I know. Who's still alive?" I considered. "Teobalt Lascari? Julian Apis? Eamon Mercutis may-he-rot-in-hell." I knew I was missing at least one damned fool, but I couldn't think of who.

"Armand Van Dahl," Mio corrected.

I eyed him suspiciously. The name didn't sound familiar to me.

"That was the last contract we signed," he supplied. "The Arborean?"

"Oh," I paused. "The one who got his head cut off?"

"That's the one," Mio nodded slightly. He couldn't actually move towards me, but he did turn his head. The look on his face said everything he didn't. I had Arborean blood in my veins, but I hadn't been *raised* Arborean, and I didn't trust northerners more than any other Calyarean did. Madelin *never* would have signed an Arborean contract. We were stupid to take it, and we'd paid the price for our greed.

"So everyone you've served is *dead*?" the masked man observed.

"It's been a long war," I replied.

"And how have you survived?" He pressed.

"Luck, mostly," Mio admitted. His expression changed. The boy had resigned himself to his Fate, just as I had. A real merc didn't beg or shed tears. They cracked jokes and slung insults until they were silenced. Nobody would know how we died, but it still seemed important to die well. "And staying close to this one," Mio added, glancing in my direction. I felt guilty. I knew that if I hadn't pushed to get Mio into our Company, he wouldn't have been there to witness the end of *Madelin's Raiders*. And yet, he was smiling, like he owed me something he couldn't express.

"I wasn't asking *you*, boy," the masked man snapped.

Mio groaned as the soldier who had been standing on his back stomped on him.

"Hey!" I protested. "Leave him alone!"

The soldier behind me immediately tried to hit me with his gauntlet again. I was ready for it to come down, and as it did I seized it, tore it off his hand, and whacked him across the face. The soldier crumpled to the ground, four bloody indentations on the side of his head.

"I warned you!" I kicked him in the ribs, and then again in the face. Though I've had plenty of years of training with both the Army and the Guild, when my blood runs hot, I still have a tendency to fall back on what I know best, and I've been a street thug since I was old enough to throw a punch.

A dozen blades were immediately pointed at me.

The masked man held his hand up, and the soldiers slowly backed away.

"Impressive. What's your name?" He asked.

"Mercy," I replied. "Jack Mercy."

"Mercy," he echoed, seeming amused. "*Appropriate*. Kill the others," the masked man ordered.

I didn't get the chance to protest. Mio gave a sharp gasp as a soldier ran him through. I lunged at the masked man. He sidestepped me effortlessly, and seized my gorget. I swung at his head and knocked off his mask. The air was suddenly cold, and when my eyes met his, I felt all the strength drain out of me.

The man I was looking at was much older than I was, with a short beard and streaks of silver in his dark hair. His nose made him look distinguished, like half of the well-bred patricians in Calyari, but his eyes were completely black.

He was a Deathwalker.

I was standing right in front of the fiend himself.

"Lord Raima," a soldier spoke up. "The woman is already dead."

I sighed in relief. The fiend evaluated me. "No matter. You'll do."

"You can't force me to serve you," I said.

"Ah. Yes, I *can*," he replied. "Now, I could tear your soul out of your body and bind it into the corpse of a dog if you'd prefer?"

I said nothing, although my feelings about that must have been obvious. He was talking about a kind of fiend called a khuri. I hate khuri. Of course, I don't *like* sylf or any other fiends, but khuri smell like wet fur and rotting meat.

"Or," Lord Raima paused. "You could *choose* to serve me. And I could *choose* to reward you for it."

I didn't look at Cecily and Mio's bodies, lying in the sand. What I was considering seemed like an offense to all the legionnaires I'd fought beside, my Housemaster, Madelin, and every dead Raider. The fiend didn't push me. He waited patiently, and even let go of my neck so I could think about his offer without his claws in my neck.

I said nothing, in no great hurry to die.

Lord Raima smiled slightly, and a sick feeling washed over me. It was said by some that the fiends which lived inside of Deathwalkers knew everything... the past, the present, and even the future.

I realized then that those stories were true.

The fiend had already anticipated my answer.

It was *me* he'd been hunting all along.

Chapter Five

—

A Case of Mistaken Identity

"Bones Picked Clean"
Ancaradis, Calyari
Fourth Day of the Month of Fire

I didn't sleep well that night. Just dreaming about the Deathwalker I'd once served set me on edge. My back ached thanks to the business at the Pearl, and my wrists itched and burned from the clawing Aerope had given me. The cuts weren't as serious as they could have been, but they looked nasty. After the sun came up, I saw that blood had seeped through my bandages, staining my bedding. I washed as best I could, and sucked down the dregs of Coriander's tonic. It was supposed to prevent rot from setting into my wounds, but it tasted like tar.

As terrible as I felt, I probably wouldn't have crawled out of my room at all, but things got very loud in the early afternoon. When I heard Tig and Rowdy shouting, I put on my only remaining shirt and staggered downstairs.

The Tail was surprisingly crowded, considering it was probably about noon. Windrider was in her usual corner with her Trader friends and No Teeth, losing badly at dice and cussing up a storm. Ferret was going over his numbers, and Coriander was sitting at the bar beside Guts, meticulously biting her ill-gotten gains to test the quality of the coin.

Four of my boys were playing Trader's Cup, a card game guaranteed to get you roaring drunk and maybe cause you to lose a finger. Each of the boys had a knife stabbed in the table right next to his cards, and Lorne had the biggest stack of coin. Snail and Rowdy had both been in a fight recently, though I didn't know who they'd been tussling with, because apparently nobody wanted to tell me shit.

Snail had a good bruise on his face, and it looked like Rowdy's nose was broken. Like Tig, Rowdy was a hothead, and he could be an idiot if someone wasn't watching him. Though I understood the importance of using my boys to run Bones Picked Clean, tangling with Deathwalkers and maybe wizards was no business for them. Rowdy was only twenty, and Snail, my youngest, was just thirteen. They were good scrappers, but knowing how tough they were didn't stop me from wanting to protect them if I could.

Rowdy acknowledged my presence, kicking out his chair, standing up, and punching air with his fist. The other boys did the same, it was their salute. "We heard Deegan Grimes was givin' Big Alice trouble again."

Rowdy got straight to the point, not that I was surprised. The boy didn't like talk, and he was sweet on Big Alice's girl Snow.

"Nothing to worry about," I tossed Tig the Trader knife I'd taken yesterday. He examined it critically, and apparently liked it as much as I did.

"You sure? You don't look so good," Snail observed. Rowdy shot him a black look, and he gulped. It was bad form to draw attention to another man's injuries, but Snail always had his foot in his mouth. He was a good boy, but slow in the head, which was how he'd gotten his street name.

"This," I gestured to my wrists. "Is from a fiend. And that's been dealt with."

As late as it was in the day, I expected that Aerope had already been executed. It was easier to kill Deathwalkers when the sun was high in the sky and their powers were weakest. Of course, I didn't have proof that Aerope was actually dead. Even if I'd watched her head come off, I would have had my doubts. After all, I'd seen her father killed *twice.*

The boys nodded solemnly. Obviously, word of what had happened had gotten around. "Well, whatcha got for us today?" Lorne asked eagerly.

"We'll see. You keep that knife," I told Tig. He grinned. I had the sneaking suspicion that he already had someone he'd like to test it on.

"Good morning, Mercy!" Big Alice exclaimed, throwing open my door and flouncing down the stairs. She sashayed over to me, and gave me a huge, dramatic hug.

I live for those hugs. The irritation I'd felt, being woken from sleep, evaporated.

"What are you doing here?" I asked. "Now, I'm not complaining, but..."

"I was just in the neighborhood, and I thought I'd stop by," she lied.

Big Alice never came down to the Tail, but I didn't protest. It was nice to see her without her usual entourage. Her dress was new, a garish combination of pink and orange Trader silk which flattered her considerable assets, and she had a bangle of foreign coins around her hips. She was wearing even more powder and perfume than usual, enough to gag a weaker man... and showing off a single bracelet of red coral I'd given her as a gift.

I suspected Coriander had told Alice I'd gone to visit Aerope, and she'd probably come to console me. A little affection from the old girl wasn't something I objected to, considering how I felt.

"Well then, come have a little coffee," I said.

"Don't mind if I do," Big Alice replied sweetly.

Guts poured us each a cup, and Big Alice was snuggling up next to me when my front door blew wide open.

I squinted. There was someone standing at the top of the stairs that I didn't recognize, silhouetted in the light of the sun.

"Hey, what're you doing back? We told you to go away!" Rowdy snapped.

"Yeah!" Lorne demanded. "Don't you know whose place this is?"

When the door closed, I got a better look at the stranger. My first guess was that he might be a bard, which surprised me. No self-respecting bard set foot inside the Tail. Three years ago, one of their brothers had been strangled by a whore on my doorstep. The murder had happened in broad daylight, which was unusual even in Bones Picked Clean. Folks still talked about it, not that I cared. My usual patrons preferred it quiet.

"Oh, will you look at that fawn!" Big Alice giggled.

"Fawn" was Alice's word for anyone particularly soft or innocent. It definitely suited the man. He was dressed in tattered, brightly-colored silks and a flashy feathered hat.

His long hair was as yellow as a lemon, and he had the most ridiculous curled mustache I'd ever seen. He chose a place right beside Windrider's usual nest of musty pillows, and stepped up on a chair with his lute in hand.

"I'm not paying you to play here," I informed him.

"And I'm not looking for money. I'm doing you a *service*," the bard replied. He bowed his head and stared down at his instrument. The sound that the lute produced was so jarring that I found myself gritting my teeth. Rowdy threw a chunk of black bread at the bard, and he played another sharp note that could shatter glass.

"Dana's saggy tits!" I swore. "My ears are bleeding!"

Tig smirked. "I got em'," he said, and hurled the Trader knife I'd given him at the bard. I almost swore at Tig for killing the fool *inside* my business where we'd have to drag his corpse up the stairs, but then I realized the knife was embedded in the wall. The fool bard didn't seem to notice it had been hurled at him. He was preoccupied with a broken string, which he was awkwardly attempting to fix while standing.

"Get out of here, you nuisance!" I ordered.

"Give me but a moment more!" he replied.

"Bard, one of my boys just pitched a knife at you, and if he wasn't suckin' on qaddi, he wouldn't have missed. *Leave*," I ordered.

My boys all laughed, except Tig who looked sore that I'd brought up his habit again. I wanted to get him to quit while he still could, and Lorne and Ferret were helping me with that.

"Want us to throw him in the canal?" Lorne suggested, glancing in my direction.

"Ooh, I'll help!" Windrider volunteered. The Traders cackled. It wasn't a casual laugh. It was like they knew something I didn't, and that made me feel cold to the bone.

I sighed. For a few blessed moments, there was silence. The bard stared right at me. His eyes made me nervous. They were iridescent blue "witch eyes", just like Ferret's. Of course, just having witch eyes didn't mean that the bard could work magic... but I still found myself worrying about wizards.

"Were you forced to come in here?" I asked, thinking that maybe some patricians had taken a malicious game too far. The man obviously wasn't a real musician, and although he'd been threatened, he still wasn't running away. He also wasn't leaving, which didn't make any sense at all. In fact, it seemed like he was just stalling for time.

"This is somebody's idea of a joke, isn't it?" I pressed.

"Mercy?" Big Alice paused.

"Mm. He's obviously not right in the head," I said. "All right, bard, let's make a deal. You can stand there as long as you need to, providing you do it quiet-like. I'll let you walk out of here looking like a hero. But if you touch that lute again, I'm not responsible for what happens to you!" I warned.

"Ah. You're as courteous as they say," the bard smiled. His grin was just a little too wide. I was starting to suspect that he wasn't as stupid or as helpless as he appeared to be, and I wondered if real trouble was coming. Ferret obviously felt the same. I noticed that he was digging in his bag and watching the door.

"Saw a wizard today. Patria's men on lookout for em'," No Teeth added suddenly.

"*You* saw a wizard?" I demanded. Everyone gave him doubtful looks, and it occurred to me belatedly that I hadn't actually told anyone the news I'd heard from Big Alice.

"Too much qaddi, No Teeth!" Guts replied, wrinkling his nose.

"Not qaddi! Ah *saw*!" No Teeth retorted. He looked almost offended.

Big Alice gave me an obstinate glare, and I gave her one right back. It was obvious that she didn't think we should be bullying No Teeth, but in my opinion, there was no sense in talking about wizards that nobody credible had actually seen one. If the Order of Light really was in Ancaradis, we'd have proof soon enough.

I sighed, motioning for Guts to bring me some Trader's Fire. "You know," I turned to Coriander. "I think you're right. This neighborhood really has gone to pot. Wizards. Sheesh!"

Of course, the moment I said that, the door swung open and four men came stomping down the stairs. They were wearing hooded cloaks, which didn't make a damned bit of sense in the heat of a Calyarean summer, and each man had a six foot pole made of pale birch wood.

"Weylan's Teeth!" Windrider swore as the first of the strangers dropped his hood.

Big Alice squeaked like a fire lizard. She tried to squeeze behind me, which didn't do her much good. With her flamboyant dress and considerable girth, that woman couldn't hide behind a Trader cart.

There were four wizards *in my bar*.

Underneath their cloaks, they were dressed in cream, white, and gold, the colors of the Order of Light. The cloth they wore was so fine that they would have stood out on the grounds of the Patria's palace, and even in Bones Picked Clean, their shoes hadn't picked up a speck of dirt. The real giveaway for me, however, was the staves they were carrying. Though to an inexperienced eye, they might pass unnoticed, I knew the difference between a pilgrim's hiking pole and a white wizard's blowing-crap-up stick. Ferret and Coriander glanced at one another nervously. All Ksrali had Sight, and it was obvious they sensed magic.

"Jack Mercy?" The first wizard asked. He was obviously the leader, a distinguished-looking man of about sixty. His short-cropped hair was completely white, and his eyes were steely and very blue. There was something familiar about him, and I wondered if he'd been at the last battle, when the Order of Light took down Fiend Raima.

"Who wants to know?" I asked.

The wizards didn't move. They all stared at me like they weren't sure I was serious.

The leader of the wizards smiled slightly. It was a look he gave me all right. If he'd told me the sea was on fire, and the Patria had turned into a gull and flown away, I would've believed it immediately. "The world is in grave danger," he said. "A Paladin will once again be needed."

"Our God has decreed," one of the younger wizards added. "The first of his Chosen shall be you."

Windrider spit her drink all over her friends, and Ferret fell right off his stool. Rowdy cursed. Tig and Snail looked confused. No Teeth stared at me with a creepy, toothless grin. There were tears in the corners of his eyes, and he actually *touched* my arm.

"Oh, Mercy, Mercy..." he yammered. "Ah'm so happy, so

happy!"

I pushed No Teeth away, but I couldn't find the words to respond. I'd never heard anything more ridiculous. If I had to choose a god I thought might take interest in me, I would've picked Weylan or Baacha, the former notorious for trouble-making, and the latter the patron of drunks. The only services I'd ever attended were for the goddess Dana, whom among other things, was the protector of whores and bastard children.

The Order of Light served Lucius, the king of the gods, the god of the sun, of law, order, civilization, truth, and justice... all things that I'd never in my life taken seriously. The last time I'd been within spitting distance of his temple, I'd been told by the Patria's men to quietly move along.

"What's a paladin?" I asked. I'd heard that word before, mostly from religious folk. During the Siege of Death's Head, the Order of Light's most devastating weapon, a man who could use the powers of his god, had never made an appearance. Everyone had expected him. The Patria's men and their allies were crushed. Those of us fighting on the other side, we were relieved.

"You don't know?" The wizards, except the old one, all gaped at me.

"Dumb Mercy!" Cookie cawed.

"Shut it, you stupid bird!" I picked up my empty glass and hurled it at the liarbird.

Cookie cawed and pretended to be wounded, although I hadn't hit him. He fluttered over to perch on the worthless bard. I expected to see the bard still sobbing over his lute, but he was standing quietly with his hands folded behind his back, observing what was most certainly the outcome of his plan. He'd led the wizards right to me, and made sure I'd stayed put until they caught up with him. Of course, before I could corner that bastard and beat some answers out of him, I did have to deal with the wizards themselves.

"Like the fiend said, I'm dumb. Explain yourselves, and use little words!" I finished.

"The Paladin, is a holy warrior sworn into the service of the God," the younger wizard explained. "It is a serious responsibility. And a very great honor."

Big Alice laughed.

"Oh, honey!" She said. "You *definitely* got the wrong man!"

Chapter Six

—

The End of the Tail

"Bones Picked Clean"
Ancaradis
Fourth Day of the Month of Fire

I scowled. I'd wanted to throw the wizards out the minute I saw what they were, and I liked them a lot less considering how they'd just embarrassed me in front of Big Alice and my boys.

Still, I had to be careful. Wizards have sharp eyes and good ears, a gift inherited from their scaly, fire-spewing ancestors. Of course, the knowledge that the wizards were dangerous didn't worry me nearly as much as the fact that they'd specifically come looking for me. I'd heard of crazy wizards aplenty, but never a dumb one. How had the four of them tracked me down without the foggiest idea of who I was? Nobody walked into the Dragon's Tail who didn't know that Jack Mercy was the thug who owned Bones Picked Clean. My place wasn't exactly on the city's grand tour.

I glanced at Big Alice. She was done laughing. Her hands were on her hips, and cheap rings sparkled on all of her fingers. That woman can throw a solid punch, and her rings are worse than any set of iron knuckles I've ever had the misfortune to run afoul of.

Everyone else had a hand on a weapon, except for No Teeth, who'd never done anything in a fight but wet himself.

I was sure the bard had led the wizards to me, but *why*? It seemed like it might be an act of revenge devised by somebody I'd wronged. I did have a long list of enemies, but sending wizards after someone wasn't the same as selling them sour beer. Deegan Grimes was reckless enough to do it, but no white wizard would work for a Deathwalker.

Even still, I convinced myself that Deegan was to blame. The alternative was worse. The only other explanation I could think of involved Fatecraft.

"Easy, boys!" I made eye contact with both Tig and Rowdy as I issued that warning. Lorne and Snail were smart enough to stay put until I told them otherwise.

Working for a Deathwalker had taught me an important lesson about wizards. Everything they did took time. Though they were capable of summoning huge monsters and leveling cities, they couldn't do much more than light a candle without a long-winded incantation. Of course, if they had come already spoiling for a fight, all our blades and brawn combined wouldn't do us a damned bit of good.

"I don't know who tricked you into coming down here, but you better leave now," I said.

The wizards didn't move. Above us, I could hear the familiar sound of the city guard coming down the street at a good clip. "You hear that?" I demanded. "You're making real trouble for me and mine, and that is something I do *not* appreciate!"

The leader of the wizards glanced over his shoulder as if he knew he'd been followed. "Come with us," he said.

There was a sense of urgency in his voice that surprised me. He still didn't seem to understand that he had the wrong man.

I snorted. "Guards!" I shouted as loud as I could, not knowing if the Patria's men would hear me or not. The clank of armor stopped, so I supposed they heard something.

"You're making a mistake," the old wizard warned. He sounded a lot more confident than I did. I gritted my teeth. I didn't want to react badly with so many eyes on me, but that wizard reminded me of Fiend Raima on one of his better days. He wasn't a bluffer like Deegan. He was the kind of man who killed folk when he said he would.

"I worked for Fiend Raima," I informed him, keeping my composure. "You can't scare me."

"I'm not trying to scare you, fool!" He snapped. "I'm *trying* to help you!"

"You want to help me? Get out of here," I replied, pointing at the door.

The wizards turned as they heard the door at the top of the stairs open. I smiled slightly. Coriander had done just what I hoped she would, and taken advantage of the fact that the wizards were focused on me. I could see her tiny bare feet through the small window near the ceiling.

"This way! There are wizards making trouble in a bar!" Coriander shouted, hopping up and down. Generally speaking, most soldiers ignored Ksrali asking for help, but Coriander's voice was difficult to ignore. If there were any stage roles for little women of such unmistakable ethnicity, she might have made a career as an actress.

A dozen city guards came tramping down the stairs, led by a square-jawed, arrogant-looking man in gilded three-quarter plate. I didn't recognize him, but he was clearly an officer, and obviously accustomed to better Districts. I gave my best smile. "Guards, would you do me the kindness of removing these men from my business?"

Big Alice tugged hard on my belt, and I almost hit my chin on the bar.

"Damnit, woman!" I hissed. "Are you trying to kill me?"

"That's the Captain of the Patria's Guard!" Alice pointed at the man with the mustache.

"Patria's Guard? What is he doing in Bones Picked Clean?" I demanded. "Isn't his job to make sure all the privies in the palace are clean?" I didn't get to finish what I'd started to say, but it would've gotten more insulting.

The captain cleared his throat. He ignored the wizards like they weren't even standing in front of him. "Jack Mercy. You are under arrest. Please come quietly," he announced.

"Pff!" I retorted. "What's my crime?"

"Must I enumerate?" the captain gave me a nasty, demeaning look and Rowdy drew his dagger. The guards immediately went for their swords, but their captain held up his hand and they froze where they stood. The four wizards were right between us and them, keeping their heads down and pretending to be innocent bystanders.

"Are you blind?" Coriander demanded. She poked the captain in the chest and gestured to the wizards. "Don't you see the wizards?"

"Shut it, sand rat," one of the junior wizards said in that slippery, snake-oil tone that made me sure that he was using magic. Both Coriander and Ferret reacted to that slur. Ferret's hand slipped into his bag again, and I wondered what he was looking for.

"We are priests of Lucius, on a pilgrimage to the five ancient temples. Here are our papers." The leader of the wizards produced a sheet of carefully folded cream paper from his shoulder bag, marked with the Patria's own seal.

The captain reviewed the papers for a moment and then turned back to me. "Wizards?" He demanded. "Did you think such a ridiculous ruse would deceive me? Are there no depths that you won't stoop to, you scoundrel? Trying to incriminate honest men of the cloth!"

"But they have birch sticks!" Ferret protested. "Birch sticks!"

"Oh yes, they are *excellent* for traveling the long road. As poor servants of Lucius, we must walk every step of our journey," another of the wizards replied. "Our staves serve us well."

"Sure, for blowing stuff up!" Coriander rolled her eyes.

"Ksrali can smell magic like you can smell the rain coming in," Big Alice said. "Maybe you oughta take a better look at those papers, Feodor."

She notably used what I guessed was the captain's first name, and his men snickered. Everyone in Ancaradis knew Big Alice, but respectable patricians usually tried to pretend they didn't take advantage of her services. Ferret and Coriander both stared up at the captain, looking as serious as I'd ever seen either one of them.

"Very well," he snorted, although his tone said that he still didn't believe a word of it. I could hear more footsteps up above and the sound of armor clanking. It didn't take a genius to realize that we were surrounded by legionnaires. "Arrest everyone," the captain ordered.

Guts cracked his knuckles. "We resist?" He asked.

"Make em' bleed," I nodded.

"Dumb Mercy!" Cookie cawed.

That was when one of the younger wizards noticed the liarbird. With a vicious expression on his face, he leveled his staff at Cookie, not the way a trained fighter would, but like it was an extension of his arm. Without a moment's hesitation, he spoke a single, guttural word.

Akhai.

I knew the move that "priest" had just made.

"Down!" I ordered, pushing Big Alice to the floor and covering her head.

There was a brilliant flash of blue, and a sound like an exploding firecracker. Glass shattered and Coriander cursed in Ksrali. The air was thick with sulfurous smoke. I could smell burning, and not just from Guts forgetting to stoke the kitchen fire. A single black feather wafted down to the floor and landed a few inches away from my hand.

"Cookie!" Ferret gasped. "You bastard, that was my bird!"

I didn't know if the wizard had killed the liarbird or not, but Ferret seemed to think that he had. He rolled up his sleeves and seized something out of his bag which sparked in the light. I didn't know what it was, but it wouldn't have surprised me if it was choking powder or something worse. Ferret held the thing in a threatening manner, and the wizards looked nervous. Their leader motioned for the others to stay back. He seemed to know what the sparking thing was, and probably sensed that my business partner was dead serious.

The fact that the wizards killed Cookie made me angry. Granted, I wasn't happy about being arrested, or having my public house destroyed, but Ferret had raised the liarbird from a downy little chick. As much as Cookie pissed me off, I would never have hurt him.

"What are you waiting for?" the captain demanded, blustering. His men looked very nervous, and the leader of the wizards gave the one who'd ruined their disguises a disapproving scowl. The wizards all dropped their cloaks and turned to face the guards.

The reaction of the guards as they realized they'd been played was spectacular. They all sort of stared and mumbled, eyes and mouths wide open like a bunch of dead fish.

I got back on my feet.

"All of you, *out!*" I shouted, although no one was listening to me. "Now!" I threw a bottle against the wall to make my point. It had been mostly empty, but the sound of the glass shattering did get some attention.

I didn't expect the city guards or the wizards to obey me, but like any businessman, I was worried about my investments. A little fistfight was one thing, but a dozen men in armor versus four white wizards was a whole different story.

"Um, Mercy?" Coriander whispered, tugging on my shirt.

I slowly turned. The arcane fire had blown a hole clean through the back wall, and a keg of ale was bleeding its contents all over the floor. If the circumstances had been different, I might have considered the new scar to be a nice touch. A wizard going ballistic certainly added to the grisly reputation of the Tail, but the fire he'd invoked showed no signs of going out. To make matters worse, it was destroying stuff that shouldn't have been burning, including a tray of unwashed mugs. Red-hot glass slag burned through the wood of the bar, and sizzled as it struck the dirt floor.

I saw the bottle of Trader's Fire that Guts had cracked open for Coriander out of the corner of my eye, and then noticed a dozen crates stacked in my winecellar. I vaguely remembered telling Guts to buy all the Trader's Fire that Windrider's friends would sell, but I hadn't expected that some wizard would start slinging spells.

To put none to fine a point on it, Trader's Fire and *actual fire* do not mix.

"Shit," I swore.

"Run!" Coriander shouted.

After what he'd just seen, Rowdy didn't need convincing, and my other boys always looked to him. Along with Windrider and her Trader friends, they plowed right through the guards and out the front door.

The captain opened his mouth, obviously about to protest, but then one of his soldiers grabbed him by the back of his gorget. Guts scooped up Ferret and Coriander, one of them under each arm, and I ran for the kitchen myself, dragging Big Alice. A huge gust of bright blue fire threw us all out of the Tail.

When I could breathe again, I rolled over and stared at the pillar of flames. There was no way we'd save the Tail. Arcane fire burned hot and fast. Even still, I wasn't about to let the fire spread across Bones Picked Clean. People were liable to get killed. I grabbed the first thing I laid eyes on that might hold water, an old rain barrel.

"Mercy!" Big Alice protested.

"Mercy!" Cookie cawed. "Mercy!" The liarbird was only singed, and missing a few tail feathers.

"Cookie!" Ferret exclaimed, obviously relieved.

The liarbird fluttered over to Ferret's shoulder, and he gave it a pat.

"Well, I'm glad you're having this sweet little reunion, but we gotta put that fire out," I said. I scooped up a barrel full of canal water and flung it on the fire. It didn't make much of a difference, but I filled it up again anyway. With Big Alice, Guts, and Coriander all helping, it looked like we were actually doing some good.

Of course, that was when the guards came around the back of the building. They surrounded us. The captain was with them, and he looked pissed. I didn't let him get a word out. I shoved my barrel at him, and he gasped as black crud from the canal splashed his face.

"Fire out!" I ordered. "Now!"

The city guards hesitated, despite the fact that they'd been ordered to arrest me only a few minutes ago. If I'd learned one thing from my years in the army, it was that in a real battle, the least confused person was always in command.

Despite all the water we were throwing on it, the fire still moved like a living thing, smashing through doors and walls. Molten window glass rained down on us. The earth shook under our feet, and part of a balcony three floors up came crashing down into the middle of the road. As the flames rose higher, they began to twist and coil. A huge red serpentine creature took shape. It inhaled deeply, drawing in all of the fire around it. The creature's eyes burned white hot, and it studied all of us with obvious intelligence.

"Uh oh," Ferret stared.

The captain gasped. "Sound the alarm!" He shouted. "More water!"

His men ran straight for the canal. The bell reserved for emergencies was already clanging a block away. Whores and gamblers who never did business before sundown opened up their shuttered windows to see what was going on, and soon the streets were swarming with people. Most of them were fleeing, looting, or gawking, but a few started helping us fight the blaze.

"What *is* that?" Big Alice dug her nails into my arm.

"A salamander. Fire elemental," I replied calmly. I'd known what was going to happen when the fire started moving unnaturally. My first commanding officer in the army had the habit of tossing matchsticks in Trader's Fire to scare the piss out of his new recruits. Of course, a matchstick in a mug paled in comparison to what we were facing. "They're attracted to Trader's Fire. Like a moth going for a lamp."

"That's a very big moth, Mercy. How much Fire did you have back there?" Big Alice hissed.

"Looks like I just bought enough to burn down Ancaradis," I replied.

Chapter Seven

—

Called to Serve

"Bones Picked Clean"
Ancaradis
Fourth Day of the Month of Fire

Two hours later, the Dragon's Tail was a smoldering ruin, and four other buildings had also burned to the ground. The wizards who'd started the whole mess made a spectacular exit after summoning a massive water elemental, which was the end of their "priest" charade. I appreciated that they didn't want innocent people to get hurt, but I was still going to kill them if I got the chance.

Rumors said that the white wizards had come to Ancaradis to get revenge on Fiend Raima's former servants. Only in Bones Picked Clean, folks made it sound like Aerope and I were the good guys.

Miraculously, I didn't get arrested. Guts accidentally knocked the Captain out cold with a bucket, and after fighting the fire all of his men were too exhausted to put up any resistance. It helped that they were far outnumbered by some of the worst residents of Bones Picked Clean including old man Percy, who politely requested that they "move along" back to better Districts. I let Windrider escort the guards home. The picture they made carrying their unconscious commander across the canal was so perfect I found myself wishing I could commission it as a painting. It was nice imagining that I'd come out on top, even though I hadn't.

With the Tail in ashes, I'd lost everything I had. I considered going back to my mother's house, but I was still uncomfortable thinking about Aerope, and didn't want to see anything that might remind me of her. I went to the Pearl instead, and Big Alice decided to reward me for saving her life. Playing hero with the old girl was the most fun I'd had in a long while.

Unfortunately, even after a good roll, my mind wouldn't stay quiet. When Big Alice took some laudanum and sacked out, I stepped onto the remains of the balcony of the Pearl. It felt a little unsteady with the trellis and the railing missing, but it seemed like it would still hold my weight.

Although I wasn't much of a smoker, I had a bit of tobacco rolled up in my pocket and I hoped it would calm my nerves more than the alcohol had. I didn't have the coin to pay for the Trader's Fire that had burned down the Tail, which added to the problem of me losing my business, but Big Alice had some of my past investments, including liquor, stocked in her cellar at the Pearl. Despite my protests, she'd opened an expensive bottle for the two of us. I finished most of it off myself, which meant that I was both drunk *and* Seeing.

Unlike qaddi, which makes people see things that *aren't* actually there, Trader's Fire unlocks genuine Sight. To someone with Sight, people and ordinary animals glow white. Black magic is just that... black, and magic is always different shades of blue.

A river of brilliant blue flowed directly under the Pearl. It was a Dragon Line. In ancient times, the dragons had used so much power to keep their cities running that they constructed massive arcane canals to ferry it around. Although Bones Picked Clean was indisputably a slum, the Dragon Line that ran underneath my District was bright and beautiful. It met with two other lines not far from Ferret's house, forming one of the points of the huge star which stretched across the entire city of Ancaradis.

I studied it for a little while, and found myself wondering what had possessed that damn wizard to attack Cookie. Was it possible that he'd seen something that I hadn't? Maybe he hadn't been aiming at the liarbird?

Still musing over the possibilities, I almost dropped my smoke as I caught sight of a bright blue spot moving fast down the middle of Deathwalker Alley. It was one of the wizards. A dozen legionaries, little white sparks of light, weren't far behind him, and seeing that brought a smile to my face.

As a group, the wizards had been intimidating. Separately, they were four stupid foreigners in a very dangerous city. Watching one of them get beat to snot and arrested didn't make me feel any better about what happened to the Tail, but it was satisfying in its own way. I picked up what was left of my worldly possessions, and was about to sneak out for a late night walk when Big Alice woke up.

"Where are you going, Jack?" She wondered. Usually, Big Alice called me Mercy like everyone else, but when she was feeling sentimental, she used my first name. When she called me Jack, I always wondered if what we had was just a business relationship. I knew Big Alice was a whore, and she could make any man think he meant something to her, but it felt to me like there was something more there. I wasn't going to admit it, but I felt it all the same.

"I can't sleep, and I didn't want to wake you," I admitted. "Don't worry."

"Okay."

She didn't argue with me, probably because of the laudanum she'd taken.

I put on my belt and tried to leave for the second time.

"Jack?" Big Alice repeated.

"Something wrong?" I asked.

"Why didn't you go with them?" She asked.

"I'm on the verge of a turf war with Deegan Grimes, and getting arrested is a bloody damned inconvenience," I replied, thinking that she was asking me about going with the guards. "Besides, I've got a reputation to preserve. If word got out that Bloody Mercy surrendered to the Patria's dogs without throwing one good punch, I'd never live it down."

"I'm not talking about the Patria's men." She sat up. "Why didn't you go with the wizards?"

"Because they're insane." I paused. "Alice?"

There was something she wasn't telling me.

"They were here, Jack," she said. "Those wizards came to the door just after I met you at the Tail this morning. My girls told me. Snow said one of them mentioned your father."

I twitched when I heard that.

Big Alice gave me a critical glare. "You knew?"

"No. But this is the third time someone has mentioned my father in the last two days. First it was those damned Traders, and then..." I hesitated.

Big Alice sighed. She sat up, giving me a look I couldn't say no to. "Well?" She demanded.

"Aerope," I confessed. "I went to see Aerope."

Big Alice's eyes widened. Apparently Coriander hadn't told her about my stupid decision. "Jack!" She scolded, slapping me. "Are you out of your mind? That woman is going to be the death of you! Literally!"

I held up my hands in a gesture of surrender. "Look, I don't know why I went, but when I heard that she was going to be executed, I felt like I had to. It was a mistake. There was no sense in talking to her. In fact, she tried to kill me."

"*Again*," Big Alice reminded me.

"Yes, *again*," I sighed. "But she also mentioned my father. It was the fiend talking. Aerope never met my father. I barely knew him myself. Alice, the last time I saw him, I was fourteen. And my mother, she never talked about him, not even when she knew she was dying. He didn't do right by her. I never could forgive him for that."

"I know," Big Alice paused. I sat down on the foot of her bed, and she rubbed my back. "Jack... what if your father was a wizard?" She asked.

"Why would you think that?" I demanded.

"I don't know. I'm just trying to sort out why the Order of Light is looking for you," she admitted.

"Perhaps I can... *illuminate*," a voice interrupted.

At that moment, there was a very bright light on the balcony, which made that officially the worst line I'd ever heard. Big Alice shrieked and tumbled out of her bed. She scrambled for a sheet and sort-of covered herself up with it.

It was the old wizard from earlier, the leader of the four. If I sized them all up, he was the one I hoped I wouldn't have to fight.

"How'd you get up here?" I demanded.

As far as I could tell, the wizard had simply *appeared* on the balcony of the Pearl, and since I'd torn down the trellis falling into the canal, that was no mean feat. The wizard didn't answer my question. He gave me an indignant sort of look, as if to say "Do I have to spell it out for you, fool?"

Thanks to the Trader's Fire I'd consumed, I could see the old man's huge aura, blue, white, and *gold* all over the balcony. He had power for days.

The gold was what really got me. I'd seen that color before. Probably not many people had, but when I'd been trying to save Aerope, I'd attended my share of Temple services drunk off my ass. A really devout priest's blessing, or powerful white magic like a fiend-sealing brand would sometimes glow gold. If the gods existed at all, gold was their color.

"I'm going to put some clothes on," Big Alice announced, more for the wizard's benefit than mine. She darted out the door, dropping her sheet as she ran. I could hear her rummaging on the other side of the wall, but I somewhat suspected that she was looking for a weapon, not a chemise.

"So where's your jumpy little friend?" I eyed him suspiciously. "I'd kinda like to know if he's about to put another bolt of fire through my head."

"My apologies, Jack," he sighed. "Journeyman Lenswer will be reprimanded for his actions. It was reckless of him to react as he did, but he believed that you were about to be attacked by that fiend. He intended to protect you. It was my error in allowing him to come along on this mission. Though many are called to serve, some are... *more capable* than others."

"Don't call me Jack. Only people I like can call me Jack. And you can cut it with the priest crap," I informed him. "I've dealt with white wizards before."

"Have you?" The wizard smiled slightly, like a stuffy patrician sipping on a drink at some pretentious party. "Well, then you should know that we *are* priests, and as such, we take certain vows. Everything that I have told you so far is the truth. The Patria's men are looking for you, and we intended to protect you from them. You stabbed a boy several days ago. He did not die, but he is in very bad shape. He's also the son of Costan Comena."

Comena was a dangerous patrician House to cross. They were first cousins of the Patria, ridiculously wealthy and well-connected. Costan himself was one of the most powerful men in Calyari. Depending on who was asked, he was either third or fifth in line for the throne.

"Dana's tits!" I swore. "You know, patricians in this city used to have the sense to stay in their own Districts!"

It made me feel better to rant a little, but I knew I was in serious trouble. If Costan didn't already know that I was responsible for stabbing his son, he'd find out soon enough. Probably, that was why the Patria's Guard had been sent after me. Of course, the fact that they had failed to arrest me for my crime would only entice the Comenas to try harder. If they pushed with the force they could bring to bear, all of Bones Picked Clean couldn't stand against them.

More importantly, not everyone who lived in the slums of Ancaradis was loyal to me. "I suppose I should thank you for the warning. You got a name, wizard?" I asked.

The wizard smiled slightly. "You may call me Benedict. I've come from the Abbey of Emeritus. My brothers and I follow the path of Just Retribution."

"Retribution? Hunh. Don't that mean something like *revenge*?" I wondered. "I thought Lucius was one of the good gods."

"The gods all have many Aspects. Within the Order of Light, it is we Judges who maintain discipline. We are slayers of fiends. Righters of wrongs. Defenders of the weak, and undoers of the wicked."

I smiled slightly. That was an impressive job description. I'd always liked the Army's *"for the good of our country and all its citizens"* bit, and the Guild's *"for brotherhood, glory, and gold"*.

"Undoers of the wicked," I echoed. "Damn, that's got a good ring to it."

"Does it peak your interest?" Master Benedict asked.

"Oh, I like it when folks get what they deserve," I admitted. "But how do you decide what that is?"

"How do *you* decide?" Master Benedict echoed.

I realized what he was getting at, and decided to shut him up before he made me sound like a fool. "Look, Master Benedict," I figured it was better to be formal. I didn't want him getting the impression that we were friends, just because I liked how he sold his line of work. "I don't follow anyone's rules but my own. I have killed *lots* of people, and I am probably going to kill a lot more real soon. I'm not the man you want."

"No. But you are, assuredly, the man I need," He replied. "Hear me out?"

"Will you leave if I say no?" I pressed.

Master Benedict smiled slightly. "I will. But I will also return, and ask again. Suffice to say, I shall not return to Lucia without you."

Lucia was preposterously far away, in the northern reaches of the Kingdom of Torres. It was where the Order of Light had their great fortress, where they trained men to become white wizards.

"Then you might as well start talking," I sat down. Whatever it was that brought the wizards thousands of miles to Ancaradis seemed like the sort of thing I'd rather hear sitting down.

"Some weeks ago, my Abbey received an urgent message from the Wise Counselors," the wizard paused.

When I didn't react, he must have realized that I didn't know what a "Wise Counselor" was.

"As we at the Abbey of Emeritus are called Judges, the Wise Counselors are our brothers at the Abbey of Firen. They are scholars of theology, history, and the law. They interpret Lucius's will."

I nodded slightly. "So *they* tell you what your god wants you to do?" I prompted. It seemed like he was getting to that part.

The wizard nodded.

"You don't have a problem with that?" I eyed him suspiciously. "How does anybody know what a god wants? What if these Wise Counselors are taking advantage of you?"

"That would be quite impossible. One cannot "take

advantage" of the willing," he replied. "We choose to serve."

That seemed like a stupid thing to say, but I didn't tell him so. Even if he was on a tight leash, he was still a wizard.

"You're not the fool you pretend to be, Jack. You feel it in your bones," Master Benedict explained. "Torres and Arborea are rattling their spears again. King Henri has lost his mind, and his bastard brother seeks to depose him. The Patria is also old, and House Logos is not as powerful as it once was. The other Great Houses are all eyeing the throne, and soon, someone will make the first move. But this coming war must be stopped before it starts."

"Hm. Well, if you want the Patria's ear, you need the Silver Foxes. They're the best in the business right now. Their captain's a patrician, and a Guild Housemaster. They look good in public, and they're tough. Of course, they won't come cheap," I said.

"This is not a job I'm offering you," the wizard replied. "You won't be paid, and I can't simply hire some mercenaries."

"Sorry to disappoint," I said. "But I am old, broken, overweight, and I don't work for free either. Also, and I don't know how you missed this... I used to serve Fiend Raima."

"Indeed," the wizard nodded. "Idun Raima was the head of the oldest and most formidable military House in all of Calyari. He might have taken the throne even if he wasn't a Deathwalker. And, by all accounts, you are the only man he never broke. The Wise Counselors are well-aware of what you are capable of, and frankly, they're surprised that you've chosen to remain in this slum." He gestured to the view. Bones Picked Clean did look pretty sorry with smoke still rising from the ruin of the Tail, but what the wizard said pissed me off.

"This slum is my home!" I snapped at him. "Your boys burned half of it down! And I've seen enough of the world to know that *none of it* is better than this! I should be stabbing you right now, but it was decent of you to warn me about the Comenas. You stay out of Bones Picked Clean, and I won't put coin on your head."

Master Benedict obviously didn't like my answer. He gave me a cold, superior look. "When you change your mind, come to Onestis. Meet me at an inn near the waterfront. The sign of the Wren."

"Onestis?" I eyed him suspiciously. "You're out of your mind if you think I'm going to Onestis!"

Onestis was the northernmost trade city in Calyari, the last arm of civilization reaching out toward the Satrapies. First, you had to cross the desert, and then follow the river through Chalceda and up into the mountains. If you were very unlucky, it could snow. At best, the journey took three or four weeks. At worst, you could be on the road for months.

"A pilgrimage would be appropriate," Master Benedict replied. "To each of the five great temples. It would demonstrate sincerity of purpose."

"Purpose my ass! I'm not stomping around the desert looking for temples when there's a perfectly good one I never set foot in right here in this city!" I informed him.

The wizard gave me another critical look. "Jack, gods do not choose their servants lightly."

There was so much conviction in his voice it shook me.

What if he was right?

That was when Big Alice came thundering back into the room with a kitchen knife in each hand. Two of her girls flanked her. One had a broom, and the second had a tiny Trader crossbow that looked like a toy. "Stop right where you are! This man is under our protection!" They shouted. It was funny to see the Pearl's whores charging in to save me rather than the other way around.

"Mercy?" Big Alice blinked in surprise. "Where did the wizard go?"

Sure enough, Master Benedict was gone.

Chapter Eight

—

The Patrician Plot

"Bones Picked Clean"
Ancaradis
Fifth Day of the Month of Fire

The next morning, I called my people together. We met at my mother's house, which was private enough to talk business. It wasn't exactly comfortable. Although it was the end of summer, the house was as cold as a grave, and it made me feel like I should be walking around with a sword drawn. I didn't see evidence of fiends or lingering Deathwalker miasma, but it was midday. After the sun went down, it was probably smarter to stay away from the place.

Most of the furniture was splintered into matchsticks. There was garbage everywhere, and the floor was littered with shards of glass. I had a chair myself, but everyone else stood against the walls.

Led by Rowdy, about fifteen of my people showed up, which was not as many as I would have liked, but some had valid excuses, such as Snail, who'd gotten his hands burned in yesterday's blaze. Ferret wasn't present for the meeting either, but his leg was hurting him and he needed to stay off of it.

Windrider was more than an hour late. Somebody had chucked her drunk ass into a canal, or she'd jumped into one to get away from trouble. I thought of how she'd turned her nose up at me the previous afternoon, and smiled slightly.

Somebody had gotten a little "retribution".

Another late arrival was a new girl called Vix from Cutpurse Bridge. I'd guessed for some time that Vix would like to be part of my gang, and I was glad to have her. Vix was one of the best sets of ears in the slums, a pickpocket who worked the pubs around the market. She was about fourteen and still had the look of a boy, though I wondered how much longer she'd be successful at her chosen profession with how tall and lanky she was becoming. A native Calyarean, Vix blended in well in a crowd and her one concession to vanity was the fox tail she pinned to her belt.

When everyone was assembled, I reiterated all I'd heard about the wizards, and explained that the Patria's men were looking for me because I'd knifed a Comena who'd been working for Deegan Grimes. I still didn't have much information on the boy, except that his name was Michel and he was the son of Costan Comena. Until I was absolutely certain that no more patricians were going to get killed by mistake, I warned my boys to stick close to home.

Windrider seemed awfully fixated on the matter and even offered to get the Comenas off my tail, though she wasn't specific about how she would do that.

"Michel is an idiot!" Windrider sighed. "He's got money and all kinds of prospects, but he still chose to sign on with Deegan Grimes! If he lives, maybe he'll learn his lesson. If he doesn't... well, he got what he was asking for!"

"Very Trader of you," I observed with a slight smile.

Windrider beamed. Because random unfortunate things didn't actually happen to them, Traders always thought that if someone got knifed, they deserved it. The fact that they never felt sorry for anyone was yet another thing I didn't like about Traders.

"So is everyone clear? You keep your heads down," I repeated for what must have been the fifth time. I wanted to make sure my orders were understood.

"I trust you, Mercy. But I don't like this," Rowdy admitted. "After those wizards burned us, the Deathwalkers are going to think we're runnin' scared. We should make em' bleed! Bones Picked Clean is our turf! We ain't scared of Deegan Grimes!"

Tig and Vix both nodded in agreement.

"Shut it, Rowdy!" Windrider reprimanded him. "If you go after Grimes right now, one of his boys is gonna gut you. We don't even have any proof that he set those wizards on us. Could be, it was someone else."

"Well, Percy says it ain't him," Vix added.

"Of course Percy says it ain't him. Even if it was him, he'd say it wasn't," Tig snorted. "He's *Percy!*"

"No, it's not Percy we've got to be worried about. Old Man and I are all right. But I think the drunk bitch is onto something. It wasn't Grimes that set those wizards on us either," I paused. I eyed Windrider suspiciously. It wasn't like her to be so sensible. Then again, she seemed to be sober. I couldn't remember the last time I'd seen her less than three sheets to the wind. I still didn't know how I felt about her giving orders to my boys, but since she was backing up what I'd already said, I let her speak her piece. Predictably, that was when she went too far.

"You should get out of town, Mercy," Windrider said to me. "There's a bounty on your head. Fifty dina."

"Suck an egg" I retorted, although that was a lot of money. "You think I give a damn about that?" My boys wouldn't betray me, but from the way Guts stared at Windrider, I could tell that he expected she might take that bait. Maybe she already had? "I'm not running from those wizards or the Patria's toadies. Or Grimes either! We're not giving up our turf, we're fortifying! And we're recruiting. Anybody that wants in, you bring em' straight to me! Oh, and Vix is in," I added.

Vix gave me this wide, innocent smile. Windrider scowled.

"This is bigger than your realize, Mercy!" Windrider argued. "The Comenas are getting ready to put one of their sons on the throne. They're trying to tie things up now, and they are not interested in loose ends!"

"Yeah, I heard them Comenas are cleaning house. Somebody got rid of Shady Kady a few weeks ago, and he was always hanging around Oleander Hill. I still think they're crazy to go up against House Logos," Vix observed.

Clever girl. I agreed with her. Logos was the strongest of Calyari's four Great Houses. Either a Comena, or a Logos had been on the throne for the past five-hundred years, and the Orias and Raimas had held it for centuries before that.

"Not as crazy as you might think, Vix," Windrider said. "Suffice to say, this little coup has been *crafted*."

I damn near spilled the drink I was sipping on. "Crafted? As in *Fatecrafted*?"

Windrider nodded solemnly. I stared at her, and I wasn't the only one. What she'd just told us changed everything.

"Why would the Traders back House Comena? They're not citizens! They're not even counted as *people*! Why should they care who's Patria?" Lorne demanded.

Guts tapped his fingers on the windowsill. He usually didn't say much, but he was clearly thinking the same thing Lorne was. It was a question that irritated me too.

Windrider was too confident answering all our questions, and a whole lot pushier than usual. With the way she stood there with her hands on her hips, looking down on the rest of us, it was as if she'd like to be the Patria herself.

"Do you have any idea how many Traders there are in Calyari?" She demanded. "Think about it! The roads are dangerous. Bandits are everywhere. Just because there hasn't been a real threat since Fiend Raima doesn't mean that everything's roses! The Patria knows that nobody can leave Ancaradis without getting stabbed, and he doesn't *do* anything about it!"

Vix giggled. "Leave Ancaradis? You can't go south of Cutpurse Bridge!"

"All right, you've made your point!" I sighed in defeat. "If Windrider is right, and there are Traders Fatecrafting for the Comenas, we do not want them as our enemies. I'm in no hurry to get myself or anybody else "crafted" into a fall down the stairs."

"That'd be a bad way to go," Rowdy agreed. There was no point in claiming to be beyond the power of a Fatecrafter. That kind of arrogance only enticed them to try harder.

"Finally! Weylan's Teeth, I thought I was never going to get through to you!" Windrider sighed in relief. The way she spoke sounded patronizing, and I noticed she'd started drinking from my bottle. "You can be awfully pigheaded, Mercy. Just think of it as a little vacation. A few weeks in Chalceda, and the worst of this will blow over."

Chalceda was the closest city to Ancaradis. It was located on the River Oria, and it took about six days hard riding across the desert to get there. I'd been to Chalceda back in my mercenary days, but I wasn't in a hurry to go back. It was a dull place. The local guards harassed people on the streets because they had nothing better to do, and everything was too damned expensive.

"Why are you trying so hard to get me out of town? Also, if you've been listening, I never said I was going to Chalceda," I replied. "I said I was handling this without fighting, and I am. I'm going to go see Costan Comena."

Windrider slammed the bottle down. "No! Don't be dumb, Mercy!"

"Shut it, you drunk bitch!" I snapped. "I'll put up with that from Ferret's turkey but I won't put up with it from you! Now, I'm only going to say this once, so I want to make sure it's clear as crystal. Nobody moves till I say so! I don't care if Deegan Leechface walks into Big Alice's bedroom and pisses on the floor! We'll get revenge for what's been done to us, but we are getting it on *my terms*! We are gonna be smart. We are gonna find out who's behind this, and *only him* we are gonna kill! We're gonna go straight to the top, lop the head off, and if we have to, we'll work our way down. And anybody that doesn't like that, they can get out of Bones Picked Clean!"

Rowdy and Tig gave grunts of approval and threw up their fists.

"You got it, boss!" Vix gave a smart little salute as I went out the door.

As I mulled over how I planned to get in to the Comena villa, I walked over to Ferret's place to see how he was mending. The air inside their little tin-roofed shack was thick with smoke. I dunked under bundles of dried herbs hung about level of my neck and grimaced as the violent, peppery smell of Coriander's cooking assaulted my nose. It was a stench capable of causing lesser men to weep tears of blood.

When I arrived, Ferret was sitting with Cookie on his shoulder in a little alcove lit by an oil lamp, peering at a pearl necklace through a pair of magnifying lenses. "Half of these are painted," he informed the young thief who was sitting on the little stool across from him. "See?" He demonstrated how the pearling flaked away when he poked at the beads.

The thief groaned. Ferret counted a number of coins and deposited them on the table across from the thief. The boy was clearly irritated to be paid so little, but wise enough not to argue with Ferret, and so he took what was offered to him and started to leave. He stopped just long enough to notice me, and when he realized who I was, he stared with his jaw dropped like a dead fish.

I knew my own reputation. I gave him a little cuff and he took off running. I never took boys who were younger than twelve into my gang, but most of the orphans and unwanted children still hoped to ply their trade well enough to catch my notice.

"I've got to go talk to Costan Comena," I informed Ferret.

"Don't be dumb, Mercy," he said. There was something in his eyes that seemed stranger than normal, a sort of luminescence.

"Suck an egg. You got anything on him I can use?" I pressed.

Ferret must have realized I was going with or without his help. He sighed in defeat. "The usual patrician garbage. Cheats on his wife. Jacks up rents on his properties. Treats his household staff like trash. Probably keeps a Deathwalker chained up in his basement."

"Well, that's no help," I sighed.

"Heh. Maybe this will be." He smirked and tossed me a coin, or at least what I thought was a coin. It turned out to be a circular piece of lead with marks that looked like claws pounded into it. They were dragon runes, and basically nobody could read them, but you saw them sometimes on charms for good luck. I could see what was left of the melted metal on a spoon next to the kitchen fire. The lead disk still felt slightly warm.

"What is it?" I wondered. The charm looked like it was glowing blue. I still had a faint lingering touch of Sight, at least enough to notice that I was holding something freshly enchanted.

"A good luck charm," he replied.

"This is *magic*," I hissed.

Ferret and I had been friends for most of our lives, which was probably why that realization came as such a shock to me. In all the time I'd known him, he'd never done anything obviously arcane, like throwing fire. He knew a lot, but it was all typical dabbler stuff, like fortune-telling and potions, the kinds of things that you weren't really sure worked.

But the charm he'd just given me felt *powerful*.

"More accurately, it's protection *from* magic. It was the

only thing I could think of that'd ward off Deathwalkers, Fatecrafters, *and* white wizards," Ferret replied. There was no small amount of pride in his voice, and though Ferret had been a city dweller as long as I'd known him, he still had a spark of Ksrali mischief in him. It didn't come out too often, but when it appeared, trouble usually followed.

"So what is it really?" I eyed him suspiciously.

"I told you, it's just a good luck charm," Ferret replied.

"I've been drunk on Trader's Fire for the last two days," I informed him. "This thing is shiny. You can do real magic."

"Well, with time and effort, obviously." He replied.

"Why didn't you ever tell me this before?" I wondered.

"I didn't think I needed to," Ferret shrugged.

"He's not exactly subtle," Coriander added.

Ferret twitched his nose slightly as if he was about to sneeze. He immediately produced a handkerchief and blew his nose. I'd always assumed that he got his endless supply of handkerchiefs from his bag, but it was sitting across the room.

Coriander rolled her eyes. What Ferret had just done was a very simple spell. I'd heard it called a "Fetch", and if knowing how to work a trick like that didn't make Ferret a real wizard, it *did* explain why he was such a damned good thief.

"You sneaky bastard." I started laughing, mostly because I couldn't help it. "Gods, I am dumb!" I sighed.

Coriander grinned. "Mercy, we may be a pair of lazy house-dwellers, but we're Ksrali. *All* Ksrali are wizards! Our ancestors kept their bloodlines strong by killing anyone who didn't have the Gift. It's not something to be proud of, but... it is what it is. Playing ignorant keeps the Patria off our backs. Right now, considering everything that's happened... we thought it best to fight fire with fire."

"Or at least a matchstick," Ferret added.

I slipped the charm into my pocket. "Thanks. I appreciate it. Let me know if you hear anything else about the Comenas, will you?"

"I'll send Cookie to look around," Ferret nodded. Though I didn't like dealing with the liarbird, the fiend was first-rate when it came to spying and delivering messages, and if Ferret needed to stay off his leg, I wasn't going to get in his face about it. Some mornings my old wounds made it difficult for me to roll out of bed, so I knew the feeling.

While the charm was obviously no small effort on behalf of my friends, I had no intention of keeping it in my pocket. Since I was sure it was magical, I had a better idea of what to do with it. I needed peace of mind more than I needed protection, so I bought a red ribbon, strung it up nice, and went to see Big Alice.

"Ferret and Coriander made this," I explained, standing in the doorway of the Pearl. I knew if I came inside I'd waste more time than I had. "It's a charm, for protection. With everything going on right now, I'd like you to wear it," I said.

"It's sweet of you to think of me," Big Alice smiled as I tied the ribbon around her neck.

"Hey, I think about you all the time!" I protested.

She shoved me, but not forcefully. "Dear Dana, you are hopeless! What am I going to do with you? Are you sure you don't need this yourself?"

"Don't worry about me," I told her. "I'll feel better knowing you're safe."

Though I didn't want to leave town, with a bounty on my

head there was a good chance that I might have to. If I did run off to Chalceda, I was sure that Deegan Grimes would never leave Big Alice alone. I wondered momentarily how the old Deathwalker was faring himself.

Had Deegan known that his new recruit was a Comena? He'd never been careful selecting his boys, so I supposed that he hadn't found out until after I stabbed Michel. As Windrider had professed, rich boys sometimes liked to play it tough in some of the rougher Districts so they could get themselves a reputation. Usually, they got punched a few times and went crying home to their mothers. Poor, stupid, Michel hadn't been so lucky.

I had more than enough to think about, but for some reason my mind kept coming back to the wizards. Master Benedict's conviction worried me. The last time I'd felt the whole world moving with so much speed had been shortly before Fiend Raima met his end. I also didn't like how Windrider was suddenly an expert on patrician politics, and was more than a little nervous about talking to Costan Comena. Still, if I could survive being a Deathwalker's thrall, a little trip up to Oleander Hill wasn't going to kill me.

Chapter Nine

—

Strange Bedfellows

"Oleander Hill"
The First District of Ancaradis
Fifth Day of the Month of Fire

I left the Pearl and crossed over Cutpurse Bridge. Nobody paid me any mind as I passed through the Grand Market, although I did get some suspicious looks as I headed north from the docks. My nerves started to fray as I crossed the river. It was different, somehow, than crossing a canal between Districts. The bridge that led into the oldest and wealthiest part of Ancaradis was huge and intimidating. It had bronze railings about eight inches thick that curved and coiled, like serpents, and were set around the level of my head. A lesser railing, obviously added later, was wrought iron, and at a normal height to keep people from falling off. The white marble pillars that the bridge was built on towered over all of the buildings around it. It was called "the Dragon Bridge", not only because it *looked* like a dragon, but because according to legend, dragons had actually built it. Nothing in the city was older.

At the center of the Dragon Bridge, I stopped. I stared out over the harbor, and then glanced down at the Patria's palace, which sat on its little island between the lighthouse and the bridge. It seemed so small from where I was standing, and I found myself imagining what Ancaradis must have looked like thousands of years ago. I couldn't imagine a whole city built to the scale of the Dragon Bridge. The thought of it made me dizzy.

Although I wouldn't admit such a thing to Windrider, I'd never actually set foot on Oleander Hill before. I'd tried crossing the Dragon Bridge once when I was a child because I wanted to see what the "good Districts" looked like, but I'd been caught halfway up by a guard who wanted to know where my folks were. When my mother found out what I'd done, she gave me a beating to remember. At the time, I didn't understand that it was dangerous to be a whore's son in a patrician neighborhood.

I relaxed slightly as I reached the other side of the bridge. I'm not particularly afraid of heights, but anyone might have been uncomfortable looking down from so far up. The place I'd come to couldn't have been more different from Bones Picked Clean. The first thing that I noticed was how lush and green it was. There was so much open space, and every house looked like a palace. They were all surrounded by white stone walls and fancy iron fences. The wide streets were lined with pink oleander. The setting sun enhanced the color of the flowers, and painted all the marble in hues of orange and violet.

The whole District was real impressive, but perched on top of the tallest hill surrounded by olive trees was the most coveted property in Ancaradis. The Comena villa put the Patria's palace to shame. His place was bigger, sure, and sitting on its own little island, but theirs was *better* and the Comenas never let anyone forget that. Before the Comenas had inherited their impressive home, it had belonged to the old ruling Oria family, and before them, it had been the residence of Ilshanna the Sorceress, Calyari's first and only Empress.

Two boys dressed in the Comena colors of gold and black stood at attention in front of the massive gate. They weren't old enough to be real guards, which made it obvious that they were only there for show.

I approached them. I'd cleaned myself up, and while I still didn't look like I belonged on Oleander Hill, I figured I could pass for a servant. I would've preferred to play a mercenary, but I didn't have the all-important Guild pin. What I did have, wrapped in brown paper under my arm was a package of very expensive cheese. According to Vix, Lord Costan spent an awful lot of his money on fancy cheese because a certain cheesemonger's youngest daughter was more "adventurous" than his lawful wife.

"I have a delivery for the master of the house," I said.

The boys glanced at one another. "We aren't expecting anything," the first informed me.

"Look, I don't get paid if I don't make this delivery," I protested. "And it is a long walk up here."

"Well, we're not supposed to take deliveries if they aren't on our list," the older of the two boys replied.

Out of the corner of my eye, I could see lanterns being lit in front of the villa. Two patrician women got out of a carriage, and one of them was followed by a boy in a blue House Mareu tabard. There were a number of other carriages out front, and a lot of servants mulling around.

"It's a gift," I added, holding up my package. "Cheese, from Lord Costan's special friend. I'm supposed to give it to him and nobody else. I think you know why."

The boys' eyes widened and they whispered back and forth for a few minutes.

"All right, make it quick," they decided, letting me in. "But... um, don't get caught by the mistress. She's... ah, not fond of *cheese*."

"Oh, I bet she ain't. I'll avoid her," I promised.

It wasn't difficult from there. The Comena family had so many servants that they couldn't have named them all. There were real guards patrolling the grounds, but they were the kind that patricians preferred, soft rich boys who were working off their years of obligatory military service in the easiest way possible. A qaddi-chewing street boy with a broken nose would have been more alert, but he wouldn't have looked "right" at a fancy dress party. How things *looked* was important to patricians, probably more important than how things were. Several servants were unloading a wagon when I arrived, and so I picked up a sack of flour along with my cheese, and carried both into the kitchen. The old cook didn't even ask my name, probably assuming that I belonged to one of the other patricians.

I noticed right away that there were lady's maids and personal guards from several different Houses scuttling around, notably House Apis and House Mareu. They were all nervous, and I suspected that more than a few of them had been ordered to act as spies. Patrician parties as I understood them weren't about having fun. They were about gaining leverage to use against your enemies.

When one of the House Apis girls upset a pitcher of cream, the cook ordered me to fetch some towels from the laundress. I stole myself a House Comena tabard while I was in the room and put it on. Someone would come looking for me when the towels didn't arrive, but by that time, I'd be gone. All I needed to do was see Costan, and explain to him that his son had gotten stabbed because he'd been down in the slums making friends with Deathwalkers. If there was anything dumber a rich boy could do, I couldn't think of it.

I didn't get very far before a woman dressed in gold silk drifted down the stairs. If anyone would recognize that I wasn't a Comena servant, it would be the lady of the house. I dodged behind a tapestry and held my breath, waiting for her to pass by.

The lady froze in the middle of the hall, and stared at the tapestry in front of me as if she could see right through it. The way she moved wasn't like a patrician at all. Her hand went to her hip and I saw the glint of a weapon, maybe a Trader long knife. From my hiding place, I couldn't see the lady's face, but the distinctive *quietness* of her footsteps caught my attention. She wasn't wearing patrician slippers with clacking wooden soles, but soft leather boots without heels, like she thought she might have to run or fight. I held my breath.

Fortunately, a maid came down the hall and drew the lady's attention away from me. I poked a little hole in the tapestry so that I could get a look at her. The maid gave an awkward curtsy. "Good evening, Lady Jasyln," she recited in a well-rehearsed, sing-song voice.

"Good evening, Mara," The lady gave the maid a slight condescending nod, and that was when I completely lost my composure. I almost fell out of my hiding place. I'd only seen her face for a heartbeat, but that had been long enough for me to be certain of her identity.

The patrician woman was Windrider! But what was *she* doing inside the Comena house? The punishment for impersonating nobility was serious, and from what I knew of her, Windrider was not the kind of person prone to taking unnecessary risks. I suddenly understood why she'd tried so hard to shuffle me out of town. I'd obviously misjudged Windrider. She wasn't a useless drunk. She was a dangerous bitch, and she'd been playing me.

I waited until the women were gone and considered what I was going to do next. As I saw it, I had three choices. First, I could give up and run back to Bones Picked Clean. Beating some answers out of Windrider when she wasn't expecting it would be smartest, but it would also require me to be *patient*, which I wasn't.

My second option was to find somewhere to hide, wait for the party to end, and then catch Costan alone. Of course, Costan would never be completely alone. He'd always have his personal guards, and if his guests weren't around, it seemed like he might order them to kill me.

Or... I could crash the party.

That was definitely the "dumb" plan, but at the time it sounded best to me.

I threw open the doors of the dining hall. It was a spectacular room with glass windows that went from floor to ceiling, massive crystal chandeliers, and an ornate marble floor dominated by a huge white rug that looked softer than the best bed I'd ever slept in. There were about thirty people in the room, much more than I'd expected, and they were all sitting down at three long tables. Most of them looked like Comena relatives, but one of them I recognized as Admiral Antius Mareu, the man who controlled the

Patria's fleet of prison ships.

Windrider was notably missing, although I suspected that her alter-ego, "Lady Jasyln" was on the guest list. Four guards with swords stood by the door, and a big man with a crossbow was right behind Costan.

The lord of the house was about ten years younger than me. Although supposively a noble-born Calyarean, he looked like a northerner himself, with unusually pale skin, a clean-shaven face, and black hair tightly curled and plastered to his head.

One of the boys I'd seen helping in the kitchen earlier dropped a platter as I made my entrance. Several of the women gasped, and Costan swore. He wasn't the only one who recognized me.

Aerope was sitting right next to Costan.

Wasn't she supposed to be dead?

My second thought was, she sure cleaned up nice. It'd been so long since I'd seen her dressed like the patrician she was. I didn't know where she'd gotten the purple and silver silk she was wearing, or the sand-colored pearls, but for a long moment all I could do was stare. Any man would've been weak in her presence, and it was that much worse for me because I'd always felt that she was out of my league. Even after I realized what a sorry, broken mess she was.

"Jack?" Aerope nearly spilled her wine. "What are you doing here?"

"What am *I* doing here?" I sputtered. "What are *you* doing here?"

"I was *invited*," She replied coldly.

I cursed my stupidity. I'd already known that the boy I'd stabbed was working for Deegan Grimes, and I should have realized that was because Costan had sent the boy to Deegan, probably so he could learn a thing or three about Deathwalkers and murder. Obviously, the Comenas were getting ready to overthrow the Patria, and I'd probably taken out their intended assassin. Costan's plans would surely be set back by months, and he didn't seem like the kind of man who liked to wait. The fact that Windrider had known *exactly* what I was walking into and hadn't told me stung. I'd wanted to smack her for keeping secrets before, but at that moment I wanted to kill her dead.

Aerope though, she wasn't some dabbler. She knew how to do *everything* her father had ever done. She could summon a shroud, assemble a morgwraith, bottle up people's souls in horrible prisons of flesh and silver wire... everything. All that had ever stopped her from becoming a complete terror was a lack of expensive supplies and a certain difficulty inherent in acquiring still-warm corpses.

I wondered if Costan knew what kind of danger he was in, having her so close to him. He was too young for the war, he probably couldn't imagine it.

"Remove yourself immediately, or you will be shot where you stand!" Costan ordered.

A neurotic-looking woman that I guessed was his wife tugged on his sleeve, "Costan, don't be a barbarian," she hissed. "You can't kill people in the house!"

"No need to kill me. See, I'm leaving!" I said. I put my hands up in the air and pretended I was about to walk out until I saw exactly what I was looking for. One of Costan's guards was standing on the corner of the big, fancy, rug. He poked his sword in my face. "Move," he ordered. "You know, this is a real nice rug," I said. I bent down very slowly and gave the rug a pat, like I was admiring it. It *was* a fancy thing, and soft enough that it seemed a shame to be wearing shoes. If someone told me that it was an ancient flying carpet with all the magic run out, I might have believed them.

That gave me an idea.

Costan wasn't amused, but before he could bellow out any more orders, I took hold of the rug with one hand and pulled it as hard as I could. It was very heavy, but I was strong enough to take the whole thing right off the ground. The guard who'd been standing on the corner of the rug fell flat on his back and knocked over a lady as he went down. She shrieked.

Traders have a nickname for well-bred Calyarean ladies. They call them "silk rabbits", which is basically what they act like. Most don't have any real responsibility, so they waste their time shopping, gossiping, and reading fiction about ladies like themselves who get kidnapped and ravished.

The remaining guards drew their swords, and a crossbow bolt fired by Costan's bodyguard impaled a portrait over my head. The ladies lost their minds. They dove behind their men and begged to be protected, although one brave girl did hurl a fork at me.

A table got knocked over, and a tapestry was torn from the wall. A drunk man fell through one of the tall windows, and landed in the reflecting pool outside. Costan screamed at everyone. His face got redder and redder until I was sure his heart was about to burst. If I hadn't been right in the middle of the whole mess, it would have been hysterical. The guards quickly cornered me. I held up my hands and sighed in defeat.

"You know, I came here to make peace with you," I told Costan. "I was going to tell you that your boy got stabbed because he was dumb enough to deal with Deegan Grimes. But now I see you got this fiend sitting at your dinner table," I gestured to Aerope. "So I guess *stupid* runs in the family!"

"How dare you?" Costan glared at me.

"Piss off," I retorted. "I know all you fancy pants patricians deal with Deathwalkers. But smart people keep em' chained up in the basement. You are fooling yourself if you think you've got any power over a fiend!"

A patrician having dinner with a Deathwalker was a serious breech of etiquette. Despite my relationship with Aerope, or maybe because of it, I was sure that any treasonous plots which allowed Deathwalkers to casually sip wine at a patrician's table were bad for all of Calyari. The fact that Aerope was at a party with the leaders of more than one House was very troubling. It definitely smelled like the coup Windrider believed it was. How deeply she was involved in the plan, I didn't know.

I turned to face Costan's guards, but I wasn't going to surrender. I'd brought just one weapon with me, a dagger that was a gift from Aerope. It had a nasty-looking blackened blade, and its hilt was engraved with the silver lotus of House Raima. I drew it and parried the first sword thrust that came my way. The second cut the sleeve of my shirt and reopened the wound Costan's son had given me. I quickly switched the dagger to my other hand, careful not to bloody it.

Aerope saw my dagger, and she obviously recognized it. "Jack, stop it!" Aerope scolded. "Why do you still have that?" She demanded.

When I didn't respond, she turned to Costan. I didn't hear what she said, but it was probably "call the guards off".

"Hold!" Costan ordered his guards, right before they would have killed me.

I held the dagger up and gestured to the blood dripping from my arm.

"What are you trying to do with that dagger?" Costan demanded.

"What do you *think*?" I replied, turning the blade a little so that he could see the unmistakable silver lotus on its pommel.

Costan swore. If Aerope's dagger got blood on it, it made a sound that only fiends could hear, like a dog whistle for monsters from beyond death. "Do you want to guess how powerful this thing is?" I said. "I'm betting it will summon *at least* six or seven fiends. Or maybe just one real big one?" I suggested.

Aerope wasn't as nervous as I hoped she would be. It wasn't that the dagger wouldn't make a mess. It was more that the fiend was controlling her. Fiends aren't afraid of anything, and even if I did summon something to tear up Costan's dining room, the fiend inside Aerope was absolutely more powerful. Working magic in full view of her new friends, however, would show them exactly how dangerous she was, and it seemed she didn't want to play that card. Fiend Aerope was an expert at pretending to be a delicate lady.

On the other hand, it was also possible that the human

Aerope knew I was bluffing.

I took a deep breath. I've always hated fiends, and although I've worked with them, I've never summoned one with my own blood.

The business between my District and Deegan's had seemed important until I looked straight at Aerope and saw where all this was going. In six months or less, Costan would move. He'd overthrow the Patria with his allies, and then Aerope would burn him dry and have the one thing her father always wanted but never got.

The throne.

A Deathwalker with money and resources was a dangerous thing. A Deathwalker who didn't have to run from the law could destroy Calyari.

A strange feeling washed over me. I got the impression that someone was standing behind me, but when I looked, no one was there. The doors were open, and I considered sprinting off like a greased-up pig when I smelled something I'd hoped never to smell again, the scent of old blood mixed with sulfur. Aerope muttered some words under her breath, a subtle thing that maybe nobody but me noticed. An amorphous cloud of black miasma formed behind me, and began assuming the shape of a huge dog.

The thing Aerope was summoning was called a khuri, a servant made by Deathwalkers from the body of a drowned dog, and the bound soul of a murderer. I had a particular dislike for them, because Lord Raima had so often threatened to kill me and bring me back as one.

I'd been distracted, seeing Aerope look so poised and beautiful. But when I realized what she was about to set loose on me, I remembered who I was dealing with. She knew my weaknesses better than anyone. If I hesitated she probably wouldn't kill me, but she would make me wish I was dead.

Before the khuri finished materializing, I charged and stabbed it between the ribs. I expected to stun the thing and maybe slow it down, but the moment Aerope's dagger touched the fiend's blood, it started burning my hand like a red hot coal. I dropped the blade and swore. The khuri tackled me, and I seized the closest weapon I could, which turned out to be a chair.

I took a deep breath and did something I hadn't done in years, not since I'd last taken Aerope to the Temple of Dana, still believing that she could be saved. I prayed.

I knew I'd done a lot wrong in my life, and I wasn't sure which of the gods would listen to someone who'd committed every serious sin there was, most of them zealously and repeatedly, but all I could think in that moment was that if the Gods existed at all, they'd better help me do *something.*

I struck the fiend as hard as I could, and it exploded. Not into a bloody mess, but into fragments of shadow that sizzled in the air and then dissipated,

It looked like the work of a white wizard.

Aerope stared at me incredulously. I pitched what was left of the chair at Costan, grabbed Aerope's dagger, and took off. The dagger burned like I'd never known it to, but I didn't feel safe leaving it behind. The guards almost caught me when I tripped over a fire-lizard as I ran out through the kitchen. The greedy little pest had its face stuffed with almonds, and it stared at me as if it couldn't fathom what I was running away from.

I was barely breathing when I made it to the waterfront, and I seemed to have lost my pursuers.

Heading home would've been suicide. While I knew that my gang could fend of the scum of Deathwalker Alley, House Comena was too powerful, even without the possibility of Fatecrafters working in their favor. After what I'd just done, Aerope would pay me a personal visit, and Costan would probably put more money on my head. I'd be dodging his assassins at night and the Patria's men during the day until the price on my head rose so high that someone from my own District would be compelled to turn me in.

As much as I hated to admit it, Windrider was right. I had to leave Ancaradis.

Chapter Ten

—

Mercy the Mercenary

"Bones Picked Clean"
Ancaradis, Calyari
Fifth Day of the Month of Fire

I caught Vix loitering around Percy's and told her what had happened. I was sure there was already more coin on my head, and the longer I stayed in the city, the higher that bounty would rise. Although she'd only been part of my gang for a day, Vix absorbed everything I told her like an old professional. She promised to spread the word that I'd left town. I saluted her as she scurried off, and wished my boys the best.

Or... boys and *girls*. Now that I had Vix, I needed something new to call them. I didn't want anybody thinking I was running a school, even if that was what it felt like sometimes.

I began to organize my escape. I started at a public house near the market and poked around the gambling tables until I found a mercenary about my size. He obviously liked telling stories, so I let him serenade me for a bit and then offered to take him to a place with better beer. Once out in the alley, I clubbed the poor idiot on the head.

I took his traveling supplies, his shitty sword, and his

Guild cloak and pin. I hid Aerope's dagger inside my shirt. It was still warm from the khuri's blood, although not as hot as it had been. If any fiends were actually summoned, I hadn't seen them. Knowing Deathwalkers as well as I did, I suspected that the blood probably had to be human for the enchantment to work.

Despite the trouble I was in, I felt guilty about robbing a Guild Brother. Although I'd broken contract and gotten thrown out of the Guild years ago, I still had fond memories of my mercenary days. In an effort not to be a complete bastard, I left the merc with his money, his kit, and my cloak so he wouldn't freeze if he was sleeping rough. A merc without armor did look suspicious, but I could pretend that I needed at least one contract to pay my smith for repairs.

Fortunately, my sorry mark already had a contract in hand when I switched places with him. The deal was signed by Simon Turova, the local Housemaster, which meant there was a good chance that the merc I'd mugged hadn't actually met his employer. Taking his job would get me as far as Chalceda, which was about a week away.

Windrider had suggested that I head to Chalceda, and I chafed at the thought of falling right into her plot. Still, the desert was rife with bandits, venomous snakes, and scorpions. It wasn't the kind of place where you wanted to be alone. There was no city closer than Chalceda, and the road that lead there was especially bad. It passed awfully close to the territory that Fiend Raima had once controlled, which meant that running into fiends was a very real possibility. Of course, I was already scuffling with white wizards and Deathwalkers in Bones Picked Clean... so things weren't likely to get much worse.

I studied the big map of Calyari in the Grand Market, refreshing the names of cities and towns in my memory. Very few people from Ancaradis ever went anywhere. Ferret and Coriander were born nomads, and they had gone traveling every winter before Ferret lost his leg... but from Big Alice's perspective, a trip to Chalceda was akin to visiting the legendary kingdoms beyond the Mist. She would talk about traveling occasionally, just to see a bit of the world, but I reassured her that she wasn't missing anything.

I'd been all over in the army and with the Guild, but a lot of things had changed since the war. I was behind on all the important rumors, but at least I had a fair picture of how big the world was and how dangerous it could be. My only real fear was that Deegan would make life miserable for Big Alice and that Rowdy and Tig wouldn't have the sense to keep their heads down. Though I wouldn't confess to such cowardice in front of my boys, I'd only stayed alive as long as I had by knowing when to run away.

I passed by a group of Traders selling horses and found where the caravan was assembling. I looked for something that said "Floria" which was the name on my contract, and found two wagons and a small group of merchants, probably a family business. There were three mercenaries standing around, looking bored. The merc I was impersonating might know one or all of them, so I stood around like maybe I was waiting for someone else.

"Hey, Guild Brother?" One of the mercs called out. She was a tiny blonde woman wearing a shirt of riveted mail and a dark blue Guild cloak, exactly like the one I'd stolen for myself. A very nice mace rested on her hip, and a Trader crossbow was slung over her back. "Are you looking for

Evan Floria?"

"Sure am," I replied, trying to sound casual. "Is this the contract?"

The lady merc snorted. "Doesn't look like much, does it? Apparently our employer won't wait to follow the legionnaires to Chalceda at the end of the week. It'd be smarter."

I hadn't heard about the Patria's army going anywhere, but it wouldn't help my ruse to admit my ignorance. Any merc worth his salt would already know what was going on, and the fact that I didn't was worrisome. I'd obviously missed some important developments that might explain why there were white wizards in town and maybe why I'd caught Windrider in the Comena house wearing a dress.

"If the world were full of smart folks, us mercs would be out of work," I replied.

"True enough," she agreed. "I was wondering who our fourth would be. None of us have ever worked together before," the lady merc admitted. "Master Floria heard some damn nonsense about a Company robbing their employer, and so Simon divided up the Crossed Sabers contract," she added.

I'd never heard of the Crossed Sabers before, but their Company might not have existed the last time I stuck on a Guild pin. Hiring a Company was much smarter than paying four mercs separately. Apart from being cheaper, it meant that you wouldn't have to deal with scuffles between your men. People who fought together often also balanced their respective strengths and weaknesses. It wasn't very different from the way I ran my District. There was a reason I tried to keep Rowdy, Lorne, and Tig together. Lorne's skittishness kept those two hotheads from getting themselves killed.

"He could've saved a lot of money," I said, mostly so I would sound sensible.

"Oh, that's not even half of the story! I'm sure he'll tell you the rest, and believe me, you'll wish you hadn't heard it!" The lady merc rolled her eyes. "I'm Lucky." She gestured to her companions. "This is Roger, and Khalid."

Roger was a big man, a bit taller than me, but with a little less girth, and a face that looked like he'd been hit with a brick. He had a real nice kit, a good longsword, a kite shield, and what seemed like military bearing. If he was from Torres or Arborea, that meant he'd been born into the family of some minor lordling. Northerners didn't have the same compulsory two years of service for every able-bodied man that Calyari did. I guessed his age at twenty-five or twenty-six.

Khalid was a skinny boy, probably half-Trader, and no older than eighteen. He seemed a little feral, or at very least, unwashed. When I first caught sight of him, he was picking his teeth with his long knife. I wasn't impressed by him, but his crossbow caught my attention. It was inlaid with mother-of-pearl and silver. There was a lot of money and love invested in that thing, which meant the boy was most assuredly a good shot.

Of course, my gut told me that "Lucky" could whip either of the two men with one hand tied behind her back. There weren't many women in the Guild. A big man like Roger might brag or intimidate his way into a good contract, but a lady merc who wanted to survive had to fight like a fiend. Lucky didn't look anything like Madelin. Madelin had been a big woman, and Calyarean through and through. But still, that little lady reminded me immediately of my Guild "mother". There was something about her that made a person feel safe.

"Well, I'm Jack. I've been out of the business for a bit," I replied. "Need a contract to repair my kit." I'd practiced that lie, so it was surprisingly easy to swallow, and the mercs seemed to believe it.

"Are you sure you want to go to Chalceda, old man?" Khalid teased. "There are fiends out in that desert."

"Heh. I'm itching to get out of town, and I'm not going to make it to Onestis," I joked, though naming that city left a bad taste in my mouth, which made me worry more about Fatecraft. "Don't worry, I'm useful," I added. I saw that he was eating an apple with his knife, and that gave me an idea.

"Let me see that," I said. Khalid gave me his knife, and I balanced it on the back of my hand, finding its balance and guessing its weight.

"All right. Hold still, boy," I told him, taking a few steps away. He looked at me funny and held his hand right where I wanted it. I took a quick look over my shoulder and let the knife fly, catching the apple right through the middle and pinning it into the side of a crate. Khalid cursed.

My boy Tig, when he wasn't chewing qaddi, could throw a knife better than any man in Ancaradis. Better than me even, but I wasn't bitter about that. I'd taught him how to throw, and every time he terrified someone missing them by an inch or less, I felt a little pride.

Lucky gave an appreciative whistle.

Roger snorted. "A pub trick," he said.

"It's a *good* pub trick!" I replied.

"Is that sword of yours army issue?" Roger wondered.

I let Roger have a look at it. "Rubbish. Lousy balance. No edge at all. I don't think you could cut a contract with this thing. What's the use of a sword if you have to bludgeon someone to death with it? Also, your blade's not straight. Got a bit of an "s" curve. It'll break soon," he informed me, as if that was something I couldn't guess. Calyarean swords were notorious for breaking, but good Arborean blades were too expensive.

"Eh, I'm used to it," I replied. That was the truth. Most of the swords I'd had in my life were army issue. The only decent blade I'd ever owned had been a gift from Fiend Raima, and I'd gotten rid of it years ago.

I took stock of Roger's weapon. It looked like a family heirloom, and it was obvious that he obsessed over it. The sword had a white leather hilt wrapped with gold wire that would have been black from sweat and grease without meticulous cleaning.

"So how long were you down on the border?" Roger asked.

I smiled slightly. "Oh, just two years! It's the same for all citizens of fair Calyari," I replied, enjoying the look he gave me.

"Smartass," Roger sighed. "Typical legionnaire. All right, how many years were you *really* in?"

"Six," I replied. "It would have been ten if I hadn't gotten wise and joined the Guild."

"And how long have you been with the Guild?" He asked. "I've been working out of Ancaradis for awhile, and I don't think I've ever seen you before."

I didn't get the chance to answer his question. The truth

was, I had stayed with the Guild only a little longer than I had stayed with the army... but admitting that still left me with almost ten years that I couldn't account for.

"That's enough, Roger. We don't need Jack's whole life story," Lucky interrupted.

"Look," I said. "It's complicated. I've made a lot of bad decisions in my life. Most of em' involving money and women," I finished. "I *thought* I was retired, but here I am."

"Fair enough," Roger agreed, though I could tell he wasn't satisfied with my answer.

Lucky presented me to Master Floria, who said he was "glad to have a veteran" along. If I had to place her age, I would've guessed that Lucky was over forty herself, but the merchant didn't seem to regard her highly. Disrespecting Lucky wasn't likely to endear our employer to any of us, but I didn't say a word. A lot of young mercenaries didn't have families, which meant that older mercs like Lucky became their surrogate parents. Madelin had taught me how to read.

Getting on my horse proved to be the most difficult part of my departure from Ancaradis. I hadn't sat in a saddle in five years. I felt it in my back right away, but going out of the city was also refreshing. It had been a long time since I'd seen the stars so clearly, and the smell of the desert reminded me of better days. About a mile out onto the road, Khalid started humming an old mercenary tune that Madelin used to sing. It surprised me how long it had been since I'd last remembered her. The way I'd left the Guild made me want to forget a lot.

Brothers of the red and blue
Sisters of Company and Contract too
Come fight
Come fight
For glory and the Guild!

Take up your sword, take up your shield
All together, we shall not yield
Stand strong
Stand strong
For glory and the Guild!

Lucky gave me a look. "C'mon, Jack!" She scolded. I wasn't much of a singer, but there wasn't a mercenary in the world that didn't know *For Glory and the Guild*. I sighed in defeat and joined in on the chorus.

We'll cross the world from end to end
And then go marching home again
For gold
For gold
For glory and the Guild!

We finished the song. Master Floria watched us suspiciously. "Are you all drunk?" He asked.

"We're *bored*," Khalid corrected. "We sing so we'll stay awake."

"No need to get snippy with me, mercenary," he snored. "Keep it down, will you? I've heard there are bandits out here."

Roger rolled his eyes. There were bandits everywhere

in Calyari, but they were more likely to attack a caravan quietly skulking along. Mercenary songs did a good job of deterring trouble on the road. It was a way of announcing, to anyone who couldn't see our cloaks and pins, that we were capable of defending ourselves.

"I fear, alas, my lady sweet," Lucky cleared her throat and started on another song everyone knew. *"Our love's not meant to be. For though you are a comely lass, I am a mer-cen-ary."*

Khalid grinned and joined in.

"And I'll never be home, home, home when you need me.
When you need me, I'll always be gone, gone, gone!
And if you look far, far, far to the distance
you will see me for-ever marching on, on, on!"

I found myself looking over my shoulder, back in the direction of the city. I couldn't make out the lights of the Pearl, but it was still possible to see the glow of the Red Lantern District.

"Oh, I know that look!" Roger laughed. "I think I can guess why you got out of the business, old man. A woman?"

I nodded. "I'd marry her if she wasn't so intent on staying disreputable."

Disreputable meant whore, and I was thinking of Big Alice.

Lucky smirked. "I've got me one of those too."

It didn't surprise me when Lucky said that. There were more than a few women in the Guild who joined up to escape marriages, sometimes because they had a preference for their own sex. Master Floria didn't like what he'd heard at all. He raised an eyebrow at the four of us but said nothing.

"What's her name?" I asked, trying to make conversation.

"Khalid," Lucky replied.

Khalid was already singing the next verse of *I'll Never Be Home*, so it took him a moment to realize he was being teased. He flushed scarlet "Hey!" He protested. "I'm not your woman!"

Master Floria harrumphed and stuck his head back inside his little wagon.

"Ignore him," Roger advised Lucky, though she obviously didn't care what our employer thought. "Some men don't understand why a women would choose this life," he added.

"Well, I don't understand why every woman doesn't!" Lucky retorted.

"I hear ya, Guild Sister," I agreed.

Chapter Eleven

—

Death's Head

Death's Head
The Sea of Sands, Calyari
Tenth Day of the Month of Fire

Five days after leaving Ancaradis, our caravan reached the crossroads at Death's Head. I saw the shadow of Fiend Raima's fortress on the horizon and steeled myself. The sight of those black towers got to me more than I wanted to admit, and if I reacted badly, Lucky would guess that I was trying to hide something. Too many good men had died in the last battle of the war, and not all of them had been fighting for the Patria.

I knew we were going up the north fork of the road towards Chalceda, and soon enough, Death's Head would be out of sight. Although the northbound road added some miles to our journey, passing through a Deathwalker's territory was suicide. Even after they were dead, Deathwalkers didn't stay quiet. The places where they'd met their end always attracted fiends. As the sun began to go down, I wondered about Aerope's dagger. I could feel it pulsing like a heartbeat, and I wasn't sure if it was calling for fiends or warning me that they were near. Unsurprisingly, when Master Floria told his caravan driver to turn south, nobody took it well.

I was almost the first to object, but Lucky beat me to it. "Are you crazy?" She demanded. "That's Fiend Raima's fortress!"

"Pff! He's been dead for years," Master Floria replied.

"Dead for Deathwalkers isn't the same as *dead*," I informed him. "The sun's going down. We're not going through there after dark!"

Roger and Khalid nodded in agreement. The worst monsters in the world shared a common weakness, and that was sunlight. Though the ruins were bound to be dangerous even during the day, after the sun set the nastiest "night-bound" fiends would be on the prowl.

Master Floria scowled at us, his hands on his hips. "Are you four afraid of ghosts? The south road will save us an entire day!"

"If we survive it," Roger replied.

I nodded, pointing at Roger to show that I agreed.

"I had no idea mercenaries were so superstitious!" Our employer rolled his eyes, and motioned for his driver to continue on. The driver looked nervous, but he didn't protest. Apparently, he was being paid better than we were.

Khalid hesitated. He glanced at Roger, and then at Lucky. When he saw that neither of them were objecting, he cursed and gave his horse some leg. Roger followed him.

"Where are you going?" I demanded, as Lucky turned down the south road. "Aren't you the smart one?"

Lucky gave me a mean little smile. "Have you been paid yet?" She asked sweetly.

"No," I admitted. "We get paid on delivery."

"Which is why we need to keep Master Moneybags alive until we get to Chalceda!" She replied. "C'mon Jack, kick your pony! Can't let the boys have all the fun without us."

Trotting on my horse, I was sure I looked like even more of a fool, but fortunately nobody was watching me. Khalid and Roger led the caravan under what was left of the outermost gate, which had partially collapsed into the road. I kept my hand on the hilt of my sword.

"I didn't realize that this place was so huge," Roger said, staring up at the remaining towers. "It's like a city."

"It *was* a city. Fiend Raima had about ten-thousand men, and that's not counting his monsters or the dead he raised to fight for him. He would have conquered all of Calyari if the Order of Light hadn't put him down," Lucky replied.

And he wouldn't have stopped there. I thought to myself.

I said nothing. Lord Raima was a monster, but he was also brilliant. After years of working for various arrogant and incompetent employers as a mercenary, there was something oddly satisfying about serving someone who always knew *exactly* what they were doing. Lord Raima punished those who disobeyed him severely, but if you continued to get up every time he beat you down, his beatings became lessons. Although he was a powerful Deathwalker, he was also one of the best swordsmen in Calyari. He understood tactics, whether in single combat or on the battlefield... and he knew how to build. His fortress was a marvel of military engineering. It had been constructed to withstand attacks from any direction... except from *within*. In the end, Lord Raima fell prey to his own arrogance.

He believed no one was dumb enough to betray him.

In that respect, he'd underestimated me.

I was still evaluating what was left of the crumbling walls when Roger stopped. "Hey, old man! Come look at this!" He shouted.

I dismounted from my horse. Pain shot from my knees into my back and I gritted my teeth. Riding a horse long distances worked muscles that most folks didn't think about often, and the last five days had been harder on me than I wanted to admit.

I went to see what Roger had found. The smell was what got me first. Something had been rotting in the sun for at least a day, and it was unbelievably foul. I grimaced, wrinkling my nose.

"Stinks like death," Lucky grimaced.

I froze. Even if I hadn't worked for one of the most legendary Deathwalkers to ever terrorize the south, I would have recognized the six-toed pawprints in the dust all around us. "Sylf," I cursed under my breath. " Shit."

"Over here!" Khalid was standing by the ruins of a fountain. There were more sylf tracks about ten feet up the road. Lying in a pool of its own blood was the dusky blue-black corpse of a sylf. Its fiery mane had gone cold, and without sparks of arcane blue dancing around its head and tail, it looked like an ordinary cougar, albeit one with very long, pointed ears and front paws that resembled human hands. The dead sylf covered with rats. They scattered from the light of Lucky's torch.

"What do you think killed it?" Khalid whispered uneasily.

"Something we don't want to meet," I admitted. Sylf are a kind of fiend, predators who hunt in packs. Like liarbirds, they are very intelligent and can imitate voices and sounds. With their agile six-toed paws, they can also open doors and even pick locks. I'd never seen a dead sylf before, with the exception of the ones I'd cut down myself. I pointed to my scar. "I've fought sylf before. One of em' almost took my head off."

"We should turn back. If something here is killing sylf, it's going to make short work of us," Roger nodded in agreement.

"Perhaps some other mercenaries came this way?" Master Floria suggested.

"Not likely. We're only here because you wouldn't let us go the smart way," Roger snorted.

"We're turning around," Lucky announced.

"Absolutely not!" Master Floria protested. "That's my decision to make, not yours! And if you wish to be paid, woman, you'll hold your tongue!"

As he said that, Aerope's dagger buzzed like a wasp inside of my shirt. Our horses pulled and whinnied. They felt something coming. I slowly turned around.

"Too late," Lucky said. She took a deep breath.

A shadow fell over us, and it wasn't cast by one of Fiend Raima's ruined towers. My horse spooked, ripped his reins right out of my hand, and bolted. He didn't get very far. A cloud of darkness rolled towards us, and I heard a nauseating crunch. The other horses took off with the wagons. One wagon overturned just before the first gate. The terrified animals snapped their harness and galloped away.

Since everyone except the two drivers had stupidly come forward to look at the dead sylf, the six of us were left standing in the middle of the road, completely exposed. Master Floria and his young assistant looked like a pair of lost children.

I drew my sword. "All right, I'm in command now. If you want to live, listen to me. And if I die, listen to Lucky."

Master Floria nodded.

"You got it, Jack," Lucky replied. Although Lucky was probably more qualified to lead than I was, I knew that Master Floria wouldn't dare talk to me the way he talked to her. I was a full head taller than he was, so it wasn't hard for me to look down on him.

"What *is* that?" Roger hissed, watching the cloud of miasma flow across the road. The ground beneath our feet shook as the fiend assumed solid form. At first, it was an amorphous mess, black as the sky and at least fifteen feet tall. Then it began to take the shape of a huge sylf, although parts of its head and legs refused to hold their shape. The eyes of many different fiends blinked all over its body. I knew what it was immediately.

"Morgwraith," I said.

Khalid and Roger both gaped at me.

Lucky laughed. It was a mad laugh, clearly stating some past experience with fiends. "I knew this was a terrible idea," she said, voicing what everyone had to be thinking.

Apart from dragons, there were no monsters more feared. A morgwraith was a swarm of fiends permanently bound together by a Deathwalker. It could disassemble itself into its parts at will, and even if it was hacked to pieces, it always regenerated. Worse still, morgwraiths could continue to grow long after their makers were dead, adding the fiends they consumed to their own mass. So far as I knew, they were impossible to destroy, but they did have one weakness.

"Morgwraiths are night-bound. If we hold it off till the sun comes up, it'll go away," I explained.

"That sounds like a tall order, Jack," Roger replied. He adjusted his shield and took a deep breath. "Where do we make our stand?"

I hesitated. The morgwraith picked its head up. It noticed us. There was blood dripping from its jaws, and I realized it was eating my horse. Lucky went for her mace, and Khalid got under cover behind us, loading a bolt in his crossbow.

"There's a tower up ahead with a silver gate." I turned to Master Floria. The merchant nodded solemnly, and I noticed that his assistant had wet his pants. "Get in there, and find something to barricade the doors!" I ordered.

I didn't wait to see if our employer followed my instructions. The morgwraith had realized there was something more fun to kill than horses, and it bounded towards Roger, giggling. Most fiends could imitate human sounds, but the sight of that bloody monster laughing like a little girl was going to haunt my dreams for a long time.

"Roger, duck!" I warned, as the morgwraith swiped at Roger with one huge paw. He almost fell to his knees, but he took the blow on his shield and carried through with his sword anyway. He was stupidly strong, and a much better fighter than I'd expected.

"Lucky, on your left!" I shouted.

Lucky swung her mace, and I scrambled up a pile of rubble, coming in high on the right. The morgwraith howled as Lucky got a solid blow on its right leg, hitting the same spot that Roger had already struck. Trying to cut it down was like trying to fell a tree. Each solid hit only chipped away at it a little.

The morgwraith thrashed and whipped me with its tail. I didn't get my sword up fast enough, and I went down hard. Sliding across the ground took the breath out of me, and I tasted blood. Khalid fired his crossbow at least three times, but his bolts didn't seem to do anything. The morgwraith expelled several dead, frog-like fiends from its body, each of them impaled by a crossbow bolt.

"Bang on your shield, Roger!" I shouted, as soon as I could breathe again. "Everybody make as much noise as you can!"

Out of the four of us, Roger was standing closest to the morgwraith, which made him the most tempting target. When he hit his shield with the blade of his sword, it made a sound the fiend couldn't ignore. Just like a sylf would, the morgwraith perked up its ears. Khalid started singing some kind of Trader battle song, loud and off-key. The morgwaith turned to look at him, and as Roger continued to strike his shield, its largest two eyes wobbled back and forth between the mercs.

That gave Lucky a good opportunity to attack again. She did some damage to its ribs, but not enough to keep the fiend from leaping on Roger. He barely rolled out from under its paw, losing his shield in the process. Roger was looking red in the face and bruised, which made me suspect he couldn't take too many more hits. I'd have to get in a crippling strike myself, and with a morgwraith, that wasn't an easy thing to do.

As I was trying to get into a better position, Khalid put

another crossbow bolt in the morgwraith. It howled in pain.

"That's it!" Lucky shouted. "Again, same spot!"

Khalid fired, and a second bolt struck true. Part of the morgwraith's left leg discorporated, and two smaller fiends leapt out at us, flashing sharp white teeth and gibbering. Lucky crushed one of them, and Roger shield-punched the second.

A sylf melted out of the morgwraith's chest as its leg re-formed, and it took me straight to the ground. I would have been a dead man if Roger hadn't seen it coming. He ran the sylf through and was about to heave me to my feet when a second sylf pounced him. Khalid shot it, and although it was already crawling away, I stabbed it again just to make sure it was dead.

Roger swore and wiped blood from his eyes with his muddy cloak.

"Can you still fight?" I asked.

He nodded, picking up his dented shield.

"Good. Take the left!" I ordered him. "Keep its eyes off me, and I'll try to gut it. That'll slow it down enough for us to get away."

"Slow it down? It can't be killed?" Roger observed.

"Are you secretly a white wizard?" I replied, figuring he'd get my point.

Right as I said that, Lucky took a blow from the morgwraith's tail that sent her flying into a nearby wall. Khalid leapt in front of her and drew his knife. Although such a weapon was better for street scuffles than going toe-to-toe with fiends, all Trader blades carried a little bit of Fate in them. That was part of what made them good for throwing. As Khalid danced with the morgwraith, Roger started banging on his shield again.

I bit my lip. Fighting the monster at an arm's length let it see us too well, and bat us around like a cat playing with a couple of mice. Sylf were cats, more or less, but they weren't normally large enough to make that comparison appropriate.

When I considered that, the solution occurred to me. "Go for the eyes, Khalid!" I ordered. Though a morgwraith had no real use for sight, sylf used their eyes to hunt... and this morgwraith obviously thought it was a sylf. Khalid glanced at his long knife, and then at the morgwraith. Taking a deep breath, he hurled it at the fiend, and the blade caught the morgwraith in the eye. It howled, pawing its face until the bloody knife fell out and hit the ground, and then slinked back, making a strangled yowling noise.

Khalid scrambled for his weapon. It was risky to get under the fiend, but with what I'd just seen that knife do, I wouldn't leave it behind either. That Trader blade had *a lot* of Fate in it, enough to save a man's life.

I didn't hesitate. Khalid had given me the opening I'd been waiting for. I charged the monster and slid underneath it. With both hands on the hilt of my sword, I stabbed straight up into the fiend's belly. The morgwraith's black blood poured down on me, and it burned like fire, but I'd done enough damage to the fiend that it began to discorporate into parts. Two greasy gore toads fell on me and then bounded away. Another sylf lunged at Roger, but Lucky was back on her feet and ready for it. As the morgwraith lost its shape, I realized that I'd severely underestimated how many fiends it was actually made of. There were hundreds of them. I killed a couple of half-formed things before I found my footing.

"Run!" I ordered, as the fiends started to swarm back together.

The mercenaries didn't need any coaxing. They bolted in the same direction I'd ordered Master Floria. Our employer had barely made it through the gates of Raima's castle when we all came barreling after him. "You are too damned slow! Get inside!" I ordered, shoving him to the floor.

As soon as Roger rolled in behind me, Lucky and Khalid dropped the portcullis. It fell with a force that shook the entire tower, and Roger helped me get the huge doors closed and barred. On Lucky's orders, Master Floria's young assistant came running with everything he could find, making a huge pile of broken furniture and rubble. When the entrance was sufficiently barricaded, we watched the morgwraith finish reassembling itself through the arrow loops in the castle walls.

"Gods! I thought we killed it!" Roger cursed.

"I told you we couldn't," I said. "But, fortunately for us, morgwraiths are stupid. Although it *could* discorporate and come through a window, it'll sit by that gate all night because it *thinks* it's too big to get in any other way."

"Damn, Jack," Roger took a deep breath. "You've done this before, haven't you?"

"When I was your age, boy, the war was still going on," I informed him.

"Is this Fiend Raima's castle?" Roger asked. "Have you... been here before?"

At first I thought he was talking to me, but then I realized it was Lucky who'd caught his attention. Lucky unfastened her gorget, showing a nasty white scar. If the cut had been a few inches higher, it surely would have killed her. "Almost met the Makers last time," Lucky nodded. "I hadn't been in the Guild ten months when I signed on with Hadrian Logos. I was with the Seventh Legion from the Battle of Death's Head until the end."

Roger grimaced. Master Floria stared at Lucky. The Seventh Legion had led the charge with the white wizards against Fiend Raima. Most of the men had died, and the rest had gone home covered in ribbons. I didn't like the fact that our employer was smiling. I wasn't sure if he'd been too weak or too rich to actually fight in the war, but it was obvious that he thought facing a Deathwalker was very exciting. I was beginning to suspect that Master Floria had taken us down the south road for the fun of it, and I would've knocked his teeth out if I thought I could do that and still get paid.

"Were you there?" Lucky asked. "I mean, *here*," she corrected.

"At Death's Head?" I nodded. "I was."

It didn't make sense to lie and say that I hadn't been involved, not knowing what I knew about the layout of Raima's territory and his fiends.

"So who were you with?" Roger asked.

Answering that question required a lie, but I had one prepared. "Eleventh Legion. Under Eamon Mercutis may-fiends-pick-out-his-eyeballs."

Roger grimaced, and Lucky sighed heavily. "Ah," she said. "Well, that explains a lot." I *had* actually served Mercutis, but I'd ditched him long before Death's Head. Obsessed with his own personal glory, by the time the war was over, Mercutis had killed almost as many mercs and legionnaires as the fiend himself. Those who'd been unfortunate enough to take his contract didn't talk about what had happened, and no one expected them to.

Khalid grinned. "I suppose if we're going to be stuck here, we're in good company. We've got ourselves a couple of the Patria's Third."

I smiled slightly, and so did Lucky.

"Ooh, I get to be Commander Gracian," Lucky said, nudging me with her elbow. "Who do you want to be?"

I rolled my eyes. "I was *always* the Arborean," I told her, as if she couldn't guess.

"I thought you looked Arborean," Roger admitted. "But you *sound* Calyarean."

"I am Calyarean. I was born and raised in Ancaradis," I replied. "My mother was Arborean though. She used to tell me that she came to Calyari for the money, and stayed for the weather."

Lucky laughed. "I sometimes say the same thing," she admitted.

"Hunh. So you're Arborean too?" I wondered. She didn't look it, but there was something foreign about her features. Her chin, nose, and ears were all slightly pointed, and her eyebrows almost non-existent.

"Actually, I'm from the West," she said.

Everyone looked at her when she said that, as if they thought she was either joking or crazy. So far as I knew, there was nothing West, except a number of tiny islands occupied by crazy dragon-worshipping pirates. Beyond the Mistfolk, there lay a range of impossibly tall mountains, and maybe on the other side, some great kingdoms that no one had seen or heard from in a thousand years.

"The West?" Roger echoed.

"You don't believe me?" Lucky smirked. "That's all right. Nobody does."

I found myself starting to, but I decided I'd rather talk to her when Master Floria and the others weren't listening in.

"So what's this Patria's Third business?" Roger asked. "A Guild Brother I met in Cydones also made a joke about it."

"It's a game," I explained. "Every boy in Calyari grew up playing it. Some girls too."

"Oh," he nodded, although he still seemed confused.

"The Patria's Third disappeared a long time ago, but before that, they cleaved their way through half of the fiends in the south. Every year, they had a tournament in the Grand Market. You had to be sixteen to participate, and if you won, the legion would take you with them. No conscription. They didn't need it. The Third had to beat off everybody who wanted to sign up. They only took the best. Their last tournament happened when I was fourteen. I was big enough to pass, so I entered. Fought one round, which I won. Then, somehow, Commander Gracian got wind of how old I really was, and he wouldn't let me continue. I never did figure out who told him."

"Sounds like you're still sore about that," Lucky observed.

"Damn straight I am! I would've been a hero!" I replied.

Everyone laughed. No mercenary wanted to be a hero. Heroes always ended up poor and dead.

"What makes you think you would've won that tournament?" Lucky demanded, her hands on her hips.

"Lucky, every boy was gonna win that tournament," I replied.

Roger smiled. "I think I understand now," he said.

"So both of you were at the Battle of Death's Head?" Master Floria interrupted, changing the subject. He glanced at Lucky, and then at me. "What was it like?"

Lucky glared at him. "We were trying to burn Fiend Raima out of his nest, and we were trying to do it *at night.* What do you *think* it was like?"

"Oh come now! Here we are, and you haven't got a single good mercenary story?" Master Floria pressed.

"You want someone to tell you stories, you should've hired a bard," I informed him. "I don't want to talk about Death's Head!"

Lucky nodded solemnly. "I don't want to talk about it either," she said.

There was a moment of silence.

"Master Floria, did you bring us here on purpose?" Master Floria's assistant asked, voicing what the rest of us were afraid to say.

Master Floria didn't respond, but it was obvious that his answer was "yes".

"You idiot!" I groaned. "Do realize you could've gotten all of us killed?"

"Could have? You *did* get two men killed!" Khalid snapped. He got right up in Master Floria's face, at least until Roger grabbed the hood of his cloak. "Your drivers! You didn't even think about them, did you? Did any of you think about them?" Khalid demanded, turning to the rest of us.

I hadn't, and when Khalid brought it up, I felt bad about that. "Damn. You're right. I saw the horses take off, but I was more worried about the morgwraith eating us," I admitted. "We'd best look for them in the morning. I don't know if we'll find anything, but it's the least we can do."

Master Floria glanced at the gate. "What if they're trying to get in now? Shouldn't we..." He began.

I stepped in front of him. "Do *not* go out there! Even if it gets quiet, and you *think* that fiend is gone, do not open that door! Anyone still out there is *dead*! And yes, it is your fault!"

"I'm sorry," he murmured. I doubted I would get a better apology out of him.

For the better part of an hour, Master Floria was quiet. It had probably occurred to him that he was very lucky to be alive. But then, just as his assistant was nodding off, he started sneaking away. Roger cleared his throat. Lucky said nothing at all, but she looked extremely annoyed.

"Where do you think you're going?" I demanded.

"I can't sleep. If we are going to be trapped here all night, I'm not just going to sit and listen to that fiend paw at the door. I'm going to have a look around," Master Floria replied.

"Bad idea," I said.

"There's treasure here," Master Floria argued. "Everyone knows it exists, but no one has been brave enough to come get it."

"Treasure?" Roger's interest was sparked. "What kind of treasure?"

"All kinds," Master Floria replied. "A huge quantity of silver, enchanted weapons, gems! And of course, the fiend's seeing stone. It's a perfect sphere of crystal worth ten times its weight in gold."

I knew *exactly* what he was talking about. "Ten times its

weight in gold? That stupid rock? Are you serious?" I demanded.

"You've seen it?" He exclaimed.

"I threw it out the window," I blurted out before I realized how that sounded.

Master Floria gasped. "You *destroyed* Fiend Raima's seeing stone?"

"I wanted to piss him off," I said.

Lucky eyed me suspiciously. "I thought that no mercs who made it to the upper floors survived. That's what the wizards told us."

I ignored Lucky. "It was not my idea to come here!" I reminded Master Floria. "It was *your* idea!"

"Calm down, old man," Roger ordered. "For what it's worth, I agree with our employer. If we're stuck in here until sunrise, why don't we see if there's anything of value?"

"*Lunatic*," I snorted.

"*Mercenary*," Roger corrected. "Does our contract have a "pillage" clause?"

"Forty percent, and first choice of the loot," Master Floria reassured him.

"All right then. I'll start with the cellar," Roger decided.

"Jack and I will check upstairs," Lucky volunteered.

"No, I'm staying right here!" I protested.

"Oh, come off it, Jack!" She scoffed. "We've already lost our horses! If we don't find something worthwhile in this castle, we won't break even!"

"I don't give a damn about the money!" I argued.

"You don't give a damn about *the money*?" Lucky put her hands on her hips, and I realized I'd just said something ridiculous. From the perspective of a merc, money was the only reason to do anything. "Are you sure you're a mercenary?"

I sighed and followed her up the stairs.

Chapter Twelve

—

Shades of the Past

Fiend Raima's Fortress
The Sea of Sands, Calyari
Tenth Day of the Month of Fire

"Ooh, look at that!" Lucky whistled. The light from her torch caught the corpse of one of Fiend Raima's monsters, a mess of dried flesh, twisted bone, and silver wire. The creature wasn't moving, and there was no animating miasma flowing through it, but the sight of it still unsettled me. I kept my hand on the hilt of my sword.

Lucky joked about everything we passed, which told me she was more nervous than she was willing to admit. I didn't want to go upstairs. If it hadn't been for the morgwraith outside, I wouldn't have set foot in the fiend's fortress at all. In my mind's eye, I could still see men in black and silver armor clashing with white wizards on the stairs. The air smelled like arcane fire, but it was bone cold.

Of course, that was nothing new. Powerful Deathwalkers were always surrounded by a certain chill, like an open tomb. When Aerope was angry, her breath would leave frost on a wine glass.

We reached the top of the tower, and Lucky paused. She stared at the black double doors and slowly reached out to trace the silver lotus of House Raima.

"You know, only the Order of Light made it this far," Lucky turned to me, a mischievous smirk on her face. "Should we see if they left anything good behind?"

"I still think it's a bad idea to loot this place," I said, not that she would listen.

"C'mon! Where's your sense of adventure?" Lucky teased, punching me in the shoulder.

When I didn't relax, her expression changed. "Jack, I was wounded taking the Gatehouse. I never set foot in here," Lucky sighed. "Still, the past is the past. The war's over. It's been over a long time."

"I hope the fiend knows that," I said. I drew my sword and stepped in front of Lucky. She gave me an odd look as I laid my hand flat on the center of the silver lotus. It wouldn't have been possible to push the doors open when Fiend Raima was still alive, but the white wizards had shattered most of his protective spells. There was a trap, however, and I wasn't sure if it had been completely destroyed.

"What're you doing?" Lucky asked.

"Checking for traps," I replied. A faint miasma emanated from the door and curled around my fingers. I could feel the remnants of the trap disengaging as the door recognized who I was. Few people had ever had permission to enter Raima's lair, and I'd been one of them.

"Ah. Good thinking," Lucky nodded.

I pushed the door open slowly. Lucky swore incoherently as she caught sight of the six loaded crossbows poised to shoot anyone who entered uninvited. Two had already fired, but the others were still tied to the mechanism which controlled the door. Spools of fine silver wire were attached to every remaining bolt.

"Wooo," Lucky whistled. "How'd you know that was there?"

"There are hidden crossbows *everywhere*," I informed her. "Fiend Raima *loved* sticking his enemies full of silver so he could jerk them around like puppets."

"I seem to remember hearing that some people got possessed by fiends," Lucky grimaced.

"Well, that's probably what it looked like," I said. "But fiends can't just take someone over. They have to be invited, or they've got to have a physical means of doing it. That's what the silver wire is for."

Lucky froze as she caught sight of an open door on the right side of the corridor. A shattered, scorched birch staff was lying on the floor. Despite the fact that I'd just warned her to stay behind me, she went over to have a look at it. "Hey, a wizard's staff!" Lucky exclaimed. "I've never seen one destroyed like that before."

With her mace in hand, she peered around the corner. "Dana's great big flabby tits! Jack, you've gotta see this!" She exclaimed.

"Damnit, I told you to stay behind me!" I protested.

I already knew what she was looking at. The room on the right side of the hall was Fiend Raima's workshop, a Deathwalker lair of the kind that appeared in Midwinter tales. The workshop was exactly what Master Floria and Roger were looking for, a place which probably still held more than a few dangerous treasures.

Although I wasn't interested in loot, I did want to protect Lucky. I almost followed her into the room, but then I felt a familiar chill in the air. Clutching the hilt of my sword, I slowly approached a door on my left. It led out to a balcony that overlooked the entire desert, a place that I had revisited countless times in my dreams.

Very slowly and quietly, I pushed the door. My eyes adjusted to the moonlight, and the cold wind caused me to grit my teeth. I stared out at the ruins all around us. The desert was trying to bury the fortress, but I could make out the barracks, the armory, and the stables. I could also see the morgwraith still pacing down below. In front of me was a large, flat stone stained with black blood. The morgwraith howled like a sylf. It looked up and its eyes met mine. I felt certain that it saw me.

For a moment, the light of the moon was blotted out. I knew immediately what it was that cast such a shadow.

"Lord Raima," I said. Really, I didn't have any reason to address him with respect... but his presence felt like an oncoming storm. Although I didn't want to admit it, I *was* still afraid of him.

"*Mercy*," Raima laughed slightly.

I slowly turned around. The fiend was dead. I'd seen him die. As a shade, his entire body was a silvery color and not very well-defined. He could have been any lost traveler forbidden from moving on, except for his eyes, which were solid black. I relaxed slightly. If Raima hadn't been able to break me when he was a living Deathwalker in full command of his powers, I wasn't going to let his ghost get under my skin.

The shade smiled slightly. "Still alive, I see."

"I'm a survivor," I replied.

"Yes. An endearing trait of yours which has now become

an obnoxious one," Raima snorted. "And a mercenary again? Why am I not surprised? You never did have any ambition."

"Your ambition got you dead," I replied. It wasn't much of a comeback.

"Who's the woman?" He asked.

He clearly meant Lucky. She wasn't in the room with me, but she was right across the hall. I wasn't sure how far the shade's perception extended from the spot it was bound to, but apparently the fiend did not know that anyone else was downstairs.

"A Guild Sister," I told him.

"Is Aerope still with you?" Raima asked.

"I haven't seen her in years," I lied.

"You lie!" Raima snarled. He jabbed at me, and if the shade could touch physically anything, he would have snatched Aerope's dagger from me.

"To you? *Absolutely*," I didn't bother to conceal my grin.

"Insolent dog!" He cursed. "Why, I'll..."

He must have realized how empty his threat was going to sound, because I stood my ground even as he hovered over me. I didn't draw my sword, but I picked it up by the hilt and poked at Raima's shade with the scabbard, which passed right through him. He swiped at me, and his hand was just as ineffectual as my weapon. I knew from experience that even very powerful shades couldn't do much more than bluster, not without some link to the physical world.

"What are you going to do, *breathe* on me?" I taunted.

Raima scowled. "I don't know why I expected more from you. I should have known that you'd never be anything but a tool, passed from one master to another. Then again, the apple never does fall very far from the tree."

Hearing those words broke me. I knew exactly what he was getting at, and I didn't like it at all. "What do you know about my father, fiend?" I demanded.

"Where's my daughter?" Raima countered.

"Nice try. I'm dumb, but I'm not that dumb," I replied. Of course, Raima would want to know Aerope's whereabouts. Another Deathwalker could bind his shade to a corpse, giving him the ability to leave the place where he'd died. Raima wouldn't be able to work magic as he once had, but I wasn't about to help him acquire a new body. Even without his power, he still knew everything he'd known in life, which meant that he could easily manipulate others into doing what he wanted in exchange for his secrets.

"Pity." Raima put his nose in the air and gave me one of his nastiest patrician glares. "Pigheaded as ever. Well then, this is how it will be, Mercy. Give me what I want, and I'll give you what you want."

"I don't think so. I'm through with you," I said. "You have no power over me."

That was a lie, but I said it like I believed it.

"Jack?" Lucky called out. I didn't respond, but I should have figured she would guess where I'd gone. She saw the open doors behind me, and had her mace ready before she stepped inside.

Of course, when she saw the shade, she nearly dropped her mace on the floor. Lucky stared. I couldn't be sure if it was because she was face to face with what was left of Fiend Raima, or because she'd just put the whole thing together and figured out that I was Mercy the Merciless,

Bloody Mercy, Raima's Left Hand, the Fiend's "Dog" or whatever other absurd sobriquet had more recently been attached to my name.

Raima said nothing. He only gave me a condescending look and vanished.

"Are you all right?" Lucky asked.

"It was just a shade," I said. "They can't hurt the living."

"Jack, that was Fiend Raima!" Lucky hissed. "You *knew* he would be here?" She gaped at me, reading the expression on my face.

"Shades are bound to the place where they died," I replied, saying nothing. "Everybody knows that."

"You weren't with the Patria's men during the war, were you?" Lucky bit her lip.

I sighed heavily. I didn't say anything, but I didn't have to.

"We've all worked for bad ones," Lucky paused. "It's a hazard of being a merc."

"Yeah, well... I got thrown out of the Guild," I admitted, rubbing the guild pin on my cloak.

"You and hundreds of other mercenaries!" Lucky sighed. "There wouldn't still *be* a Guild in Calyari if they hadn't issued a general amnesty."

I hadn't known about the Guild reinstating mercs who'd fought for Raima, but that didn't matter. I was sure that such forgiveness was meant for the companies who'd patrolled the roads or sat guard duty. It wouldn't be extended to someone like me.

"So what did the fiend want?" Lucky asked. "I heard him say something about your father."

I sighed. Part of me wanted to tell Lucky my whole story.

Ferret was my usual source of advice, and since leaving Ancaradis I'd come up with an awful lot of questions I wanted to ask someone. Lucky was smart, and I wondered if she could help set my mind at ease.

"It's complicated, and to be honest I don't know the half of it. My father was a soldier. Never around much. He disappeared for good when I was... twelve, or fourteen. I don't remember. But lately it seems that *everyone* is connecting him to me! Some damn fools burned my public house to the ground last week, and before that, I stabbed a rich boy whose father put a price on my head. That's what really got me back into this business. Everything else was a lie."

Lucky nodded. "I've heard a lot of Madelin's Raiders stories from Simon Turova. He let it slip once that him and Jean weren't the only survivors of the Company still in Ancaradis. I get the impression he doesn't like you much."

"Simon didn't like me when I *was* a Raider," I informed her. "And he was laid up at the Colona Guildhouse with a broken arm when the rest of us were at the Vermillion River, so whatever stories he's telling these days are probably shit. Right now, I'm in something bad, and I don't know what it is. Might be a plot to overthrow the Patria, or it might be bigger than that. Two real powerful fiends have now told me that I'm just like my old man, and they don't seem to like him much. My woman Alice thinks that maybe my father's a white wizard. Could explain why everyone's so interested in him. And me. I don't figure I'm Gifted though. I only have Sight when I'm drunk on Trader's Fire."

"Don't wizards take a vow of celibacy?" Lucky wondered.

"That seems like the kind of vow a lot of men would break," I said.

Lucky agreed. "Women too. Weylan knows I couldn't do it," she laughed slightly, mostly to break the silence. She also seemed distracted. Her gaze kept drifting back to the spot where Fiend Raima had appeared.

"We should go before that shade comes back," I said. "He might not be able to hurt us, but if I talk to him too long, I might tell him things I shouldn't," I confessed.

Lucky hesitated.

"What are you thinking? Spit it out," I ordered.

"Well, you know, there are lots of mercs who *claim* to be students of Savin Raima's school, but they're full of it," Lucky said.

I smiled slightly. I knew exactly what she was asking. Before Fiend Raima came along, his grandfather Savin had been the most famous member of the family. Without a doubt, he was the greatest swordsman in the history of Calyari.

"What makes you think I know anything?" I asked.

Lucky grinned. "I don't think you know *anything*, old man. I think you know *everything*."

"Well, Lord Raima was a bastard, don't get me wrong. But he could kill folk, and he could do it in ways that made you very nervous about crossing him," I admitted. "And... well, if I hadn't picked up a few tricks, I'd be dead."

"I'm getting old," Lucky replied. "I need some new tricks myself."

"You should know, if people see you cutting down fiends like a Deathwalker, they're going to think certain things," I paused. "Like maybe you're not such a nice merc."

"I'd rather be a live merc than a nice one," Lucky admitted. "Anyway, isn't it best to fight fire with fire?"

I immediately thought of Ferret. "It'll be more like fighting fire with a matchstick. I'm rusty."

Lucky wasn't convinced. She put her hands on her hips and gave me a look that reminded me of my mother, or maybe Madelin.

"All right," I agreed. "We've got a few more days until Chalceda. I'll show you some things from the *real* Raima School. But you've got to keep quiet about this!" I warned.

"My lips are sealed," Lucky vowed. "Although Roger did watch you dice up that morgwraith, and he's sharper than he looks."

"Roger I can deal with," I shrugged. "Master Floria is the problem. I was against coming down here because I knew something like this would happen. I don't want him thinking everything was my fault."

"You want paid," Lucky observed.

"Obviously," I replied.

She elbowed me with a smile. "Hah! There you go! I knew you were a mercenary!"

Chapter Thirteen

—

Legacies and Lies

The Road to Chalceda
The Sea of Sands, Calyari
Eleventh Day of the Month of Fire

When the sun came up, I still hadn't slept. The morgwraith was gone. Roger's nose looked bad, and the rest of us were covered in cuts and bruises. Master Floria seemed complacent, if annoyed that he'd found no sign of Fiend Raima's seeing stone.

Of course, I'd destroyed it exactly as I'd said. At the time, I hadn't known that the stupid thing was worth ten times its weight in gold. I might have thrown it out the window anyway, if only to see the fiend's reaction when it shattered.

Scouring the ruins, we managed to find one of Master Floria's drivers who'd spent the night in a cistern with a broken arm, one mule, and Khalid's good little Trader pony. Most of Master Floria's goods were silks, which had been well-packed and had fared surprisingly well for being tossed around by the morgwraith. We packed as much as we could into our remaining wagon, hitched up Khalid's pony, and stowed everything else inside the fortress.

Roger reassured Master Floria that he could probably send someone back for the remainder of the goods, so long as they came in the morning and left before dark. Chalceda was less than two days away, and a strong Company would take the contract, provided that the price was high enough. Master Floria's response surprised me. He stated simply that he would prefer never to see the fortress again, and then added that he had already lost all of the money he'd intended to pay us. There was also the price he'd have to pay to the family of the dead caravan driver, which was likely to be steep.

Lucky said nothing at all, but I knew she was going to tell the Guild about Master Floria's reckless behavior. Mercs got hazard pay if they knew they'd be fighting fiends, and if an employer wanted to travel a route known to be unsafe, the rate per day was twice as expensive. The Guild's rules were strict, but they were strict for good reason. Too many employers thought of mercenaries as expendable, which was not an attitude that the Guild wanted to encourage.

Once Lord Raima's fortress was well out of sight, the four of us mercs got to talking about our situation.

"Is Master Floria really not going to pay us?" Khalid wondered.

"Oh, he'll pay us!" I replied. "If we don't break contract before we get to Chalceda, he has to. He either pays, or he goes to prison."

Khalid laughed. "That silk rabbit wouldn't last a day in prison," he said. Khalid had been to prison before. His tone convinced me of that.

"That's why he's going to pay," I replied. I had some experience with prison myself.

"He's also going to get fined," Lucky added. "My Housemaster will hammer him for this one, and so will yours."

I realized Lucky was talking to me, and I nodded. Simon would be furious when he discovered that I was pretending to work for him. But, as a former Raider, I knew he'd be more upset about how Master Floria had ignored the warnings of the mercenaries he'd hired and almost gotten all of us killed.

"Ol' Bill sure does love his money," Lucky continued. "That's why Onestis is one of the richest Guild Houses in Calyari. My Housemaster doesn't let his Brothers and Sisters get taken advantage of."

"Floria will be lucky if he isn't blacklisted," Roger added. "It'll take a month for me to get word to Bastion, but my Housemaster won't like this either. And four complaints from four different Guild Houses is a lot of marks against someone."

"He should've hired that Company," I said.

Lucky rolled her eyes. "I don't know, Jack. I like the Crossed Sabers, but those boys might not have made it through there."

"*We* wouldn't have made it if it hadn't been for you," Roger added, his eyes boring holes in my head.

I didn't respond to that.

"So I should make a formal complaint too?" Khalid asked, breaking the uncomfortable silence. "I've never had to do that before," he admitted.

"Don't worry. I'll help you get it written," Lucky offered. "It'll be perfectly horrible. You might even get paid double."

"*Double*?" Khalid gasped. He stared at her in disbelief.

Of course, Master Floria was far enough behind us that he couldn't have heard what we were saying about him. As

Roger explained the particulars of Guild fines and fees to Khalid, I plodded ahead. Lucky followed after me.

"You're sure in a hurry," she observed.

"We've got to make up time now that we're walking to Chalceda," I replied.

"We'll get there when we get there," Lucky shrugged.

"No, I've got another contract," I lied. "I don't want to miss it."

"Where are you going?" Lucky asked.

I hesitated. I didn't have a place in mind, and when I tried to remember the large map of Calyari in the market, I couldn't envision the names of any of the cities near Chalceda. "Onestis," I said, before I remembered that was where Lucky's Guild House was located. And of course, that was where Master Benedict had promised to meet me.

"Hah! I'm going that way myself," Lucky grinned. "Maybe we can travel together?"

"I don't think my employer wants to pay two mercs," I shrugged.

"Well, certainly don't tell him so, but I'll come for free. To tell the truth, I'm a little nervous," Lucky admitted. "Mercs have been disappearing on the north road recently. You know, if you do miss your contract, maybe Housemaster Yuri will pay the two of us to investigate."

"Eh, maybe?" I shrugged. I had no intention of actually going to Onestis, but the idea of mercenaries disappearing worried me. I thought of the white wizards again, and shuddered. Not for the first time, I wondered if the Traders involved in the whole Comena business were also crafting my Fate.

"Why do you want to travel with me anyway?" I teased,

elbowing Lucky. "I'm a scumbag."

"Oh, sure you are!" Lucky replied. "You're not a scumbag, Jack. You're a big softie. And from what I saw, I'm pretty sure that if Fiend Raima wasn't dead, he'd love to kill you. What did you do to him? Besides destroy his magic rock?"

"I ran off with his daughter," I replied.

"Disreputable woman?" Lucky teased.

I smiled slightly. "The worst. Not a whore, but beautiful, brilliant, and *crazy*."

"Wait, you're serious?" Lucky grinned. "You ran off with Fiend Raima's *daughter*?"

"We saw the white wizards get through the gatehouse," I replied, smiling slightly myself. "And we may have forgotten to lock a few doors as we went out the back."

"*That* is amazing! Practically a Midwinter's tale!" Lucky declared, slapping me on the back. "When we get to Chalceda, I'm buying you a drink. Or... several drinks. One for saving my life, and however many it takes for you to tell me how you seduced the Deathlord's beautiful daughter! I want to hear it from the beginning!"

"All right," I smiled slightly. It had been the other way around if I was honest about it. I'd avoided Aerope at first, knowing how dangerous she was. Of course, that had only enticed her to try harder.

I watched Lucky trudging through the sand, just ahead of me. I liked her, but I couldn't take her offer of friendship. I hadn't thought about my mercenary days in a long while, and I realized I'd never actually sat down and raised a glass to Madelin or any of the other dead Raiders. Saluting a fallen merc was something that Guild Brothers and Sisters did together, and it didn't seem right to drag Lucky into the mess I was in. Sooner or later, word would get out about the Guild Brother I'd robbed back in Ancaradis.

I liked being a mercenary, but I didn't deserve to be one.

We made it to the River Oria, and were only about fifteen miles from Chalceda when we passed a few Traders on the road. They were surprised to see four mercs caked in sand, walking across the desert instead of riding. They wanted to know what happened to our horses, and tried to sell us two old nags, which Master Floria refused to buy. After we told our story, the Traders agreed to retrieve everything we'd left in Raima's fortress if they could help themselves to some of the loot. Master Floria agreed to their terms and informed the four of us that Traders were "cheaper than mercenaries".

None off us said anything, although from the way Khalid watched Master Floria, it was obvious that he knew we were being conned. The Traders would make it to Lord Raima's fortress without trouble, and I didn't doubt their ability to avoid the fiends. They weren't dumb enough to go into ruins after dark, and they'd probably have their safety Fatecrafted. Of course, once they got what they wanted, they'd disappear and Master Floria would never see the rest of his goods again.

A woman riding with the Traders looked familiar to me, but I didn't say anything to her. The only thing worse than being involved in a Trader plot was letting them know you were wise to their plans.

We stopped to rest for a bit, and watered the animals at the river. Master Floria was anxious to do a full accounting of what the mess we were in had cost him before he arrived in Chalceda and had to explain it to his business partners. The rest of us were given leave to do whatever we wanted for a few hours, provided that we all kept our eyes open.

Khalid promptly fell asleep under a tree, and Roger put together a makeshift fishing pole to see if he could catch something worth eating.

Lucky and I had plans.

I handed her a short stick. "This is your sword," I said.

She glanced at it doubtfully. "Can't I use your sword?"

"Not until you know what's going to happen," I smiled slightly. "Now come at me."

"Don't you need a weapon?" She asked.

"I don't," I replied. "That's the point of this technique."

"All right, you asked for it," Lucky nodded. As I guessed she would, Lucky charged in straight. It was army training, and it worked well enough when you were fighting other people who'd learned to fight the same way. Street fighting was all circles and not lines. Despite the fact that Savin Raima was a patrician, his fighting style combined dirty tricks used by Traders and Ksrali with things he'd witnessed secretly prowling the worst streets of Ancaradis. I stepped out, blocking Lucky's sword hand on my forearm. Then I brought my other hand up under her arm, just above her elbow and kicked her legs out from under her. By the time she realized what I was about to do, she was on her back.

"Ooo!" Lucky stared up at the sky. "What just happened?" She wondered.

"I took your sword and I killed you with it," I replied, pointing the stick at her throat.

"All right. Let's see that again," she decided, climbing back to her feet.

We went over the technique several more times, and then I snapped her stick in half. "It's the same thing with a knife," I explained. "But you'll have to get closer if you intend to stab me, so it's going to feel different." I demonstrated. "You see a lot of stupid people swing real wide with knives. Never do that. Get up close, give the man a hug, and put your blade right between his ribs. Shove him against a wall with your forearm, cover up his mouth so he can't scream, and then twist the knife up if you want him to bleed out quicker."

Lucky grimaced.

"You practice it enough, and you won't even have to think about it," I finished, although that was exactly what had gotten me into trouble with House Comena.

We continued working until it was almost time to pick up and carry on, and by then we were both soaked with sweat.

"Do you want to see one more?" I suggested. I'd saved my favorite trick for last and was looking forward to showing it off.

"Oh, I'm done, old man," Lucky shook her head.

"Old man? I'll take that from Roger and Khalid, but not from you!" I argued. "How old are you anyway?"

"Never ask a lady that!" She gasped in mock horror.

"So thirty-eight? Forty?" I taunted.

"No!" She punched me in the shoulder. "Twenty-nine! Always and forever!"

I laughed and wiped sweat from my face on the sleeve of my shirt. That was when Roger came forward. Apparently he hadn't fared well with his fishing, or something else was getting to him. He seemed unusually edgy.

"This man is a fiend!" Lucky declared, shoving me.

"Getting a little training in, eh?" Roger observed.

"Just a couple of tricks," I shrugged.

"Those are some "tricks", Jack," Roger replied. I realized he'd been watching us all along. "You're very good at killing people. Fiends too. Have you ever given any thought to taking House post? People come to the Guild all the time wanting to learn to fight, but few mercs know how to do more than keep themselves alive."

I shrugged. "If you want the truth, that's all I know how to do."

"No, you have a style, although it's not one I've seen before. The way you circle. It's *distinctive*. It's been drilled into you. I saw it a bit when we were up against that fiend. I'd like to see it again in daylight," Roger admitted.

"I'm tired," I said.

"You just asked Lucky if she wanted to go another round," he reminded me.

"All right, fine," I sighed. I picked up another stick, but Roger tossed me my sword.

Our blades clashed, and I immediately got the impression that he wanted to fight, not just to see my skills, but to actually beat me.

"Damnit, Roger! What are you trying to do?" I demanded. He didn't answer.

He was damn strong, and I had to dig my heels into the ground to prevent him from knocking me flat on my back. Roger drew back, and then charged. Without thinking, I immediately knocked him down with the same nasty, elegant move I'd been teaching Lucky. The difference was, when we'd been working with a stick, I hadn't hit her hard enough to separate her shoulder. But when Roger charged at me without hesitation, I did just that.

He swore and dropped his blade, clutching his injury.

"Shit, I'm sorry. Why did you come at me so fast?" I moved to help him up, but I didn't get close enough. He was back on his feet in a heartbeat and drew his a dagger from his boot. He pointed the blade at me.

"Take it easy! It was an accident!" I held my hands up in a gesture of surrender.

Roger laughed. It was a harsh croaking sound which suggested that he didn't really think anything was funny and had basically lost his head. He was fumbling for something wrapped in layers of bandages, and I almost punched him when I saw that it was Aerope's dagger.

"You *went through my pack*?"

Lucky gave a low whistle, and Khalid also looked surprised. A Guild Brother's "pack" was sacred. No merc went through another merc's personal belongings without permission. In any case, the damage had been done. Aerope's dagger was out in the open, and that meant my ruse was up. I found myself wishing I'd thrown the blade in a canal before I'd left Ancaradis.

"You're Bloody Mercy," Roger said. "Fiend Raima's bodyguard."

"The fiend's dead," I reminded him. "I don't serve him anymore."

Though Lucky already knew that I'd worked for Raima, she gave me a surprised look. Now that I was unmasked, she was obviously going to pretend that she didn't know what was going on. I didn't blame her. If our positions had been reversed, I might have done the same thing. Khalid stared with his jaw dropped, and Master Floria gasped.

"I heard about you back in Ancaradis, a big thug running a little slum," Roger continued. "I thought it was all talk until I saw you fight. And this weapon proves it."

"Is that what I think it is?" Master Floria stared at Aerope's dagger.

"A summoning dagger. It has the insignia of House Raima on it. And it's been cleaned recently," Roger said.

"You made that fiend attack us?" Master Floria gasped.

"No," I protested. "I did *not* summon that morgwraith! You *can't* summon one of those with a dagger! Yes, I cleaned the blade... but that's because I killed a khuri with it *before* I left Ancaradis. I'm not a Deathwalker! Look at my eyes!"

For a moment, no one said anything. My eyes are gray, with just a little hint of blue. Although they don't have the shimmer of a wizard's, it would've made more sense to accuse me of being a witch than a Deathwalker.

"But you served Fiend Raima?" Khalid asked.

"So did a lot of other people who didn't want their heads on pikes!" I argued. "I've got no love for that fiend! *None!*"

"Why'd you keep his dagger then?" Roger pressed. Of course, I had no honest answer to that question. I'd started telling Lucky about my relationship with Aerope, but it was obvious that Roger wasn't going to care about that story. In fact, I got the distinct impression that if I hadn't dislocated his shoulder, he'd still be trying to kill me.

Master Floria gave me a wide berth when I glanced in his direction, and I decided I was done trying to explain myself.

"You know what? We're close enough to Chalceda. I'm

done," I took off my mercenary pin and threw it at Roger. When he fumbled for it, I seized Aerope's dagger, and tucked it right in my belt where everyone could see it.

"Jack!" Lucky tried to stop me from leaving, but I brushed her off.

"I like you, Lucky, but I'm not putting up with this!" I told her, and she clammed right up. She still looked obstinate though, and if I spent any longer standing around, I suspected she'd start trying to lecture me about quitting contracts because of one stupid scuffle.

I didn't take two steps before something hit me hard across the back of the head. I crumpled to the ground like I didn't have a bone in my body, everything red and just full of pain.

As I struggled to stay conscious, I could hear Lucky was screaming at Master Floria. There was a lot of blood in the sand under my nose. It seemed to be coming from the back of my head, but I still didn't know if it had been a sword or a rock. I was reasonably sure I was dying, but there wasn't anything I could do.

It had been stupid of me to think that I could just run back to the Guild and be accepted. Helping the white wizards kill Lord Raima hadn't been enough to clean my slate. The fiend knew I wasn't free of him. Sometimes I wished I was still under his thumb so I could just follow orders and never make any decisions at all.

Although I knew that most of what Raima had done was evil, I found myself missing the old bastard. Even if he appeared to lose, he always had the foresight to prepare a loophole that he could later exploit. He wouldn't have been so stupid as to turn his back on a man that had tried to kill him not ten minutes ago.

The last thing I saw before I lost consciousness was Roger looming over me and taking both my Guild pin, and Aerope's dagger from my belt.

Chapter Fourteen

—

The Fiend's Dog

Fiend Raima's Fortress
The Sea of Sands, Calyari
27th Year of the reign of Patria Theodas Logos IV

Seven Years Ago

I stared at the fiend. It was a baggorth made of flesh and silver wire, sewn and re-sewn more times than I could count. Lord Raima had fashioned it to be used as a cutting target, and every part of it was ridiculously strong. Only a perfect blow would take it down, and I couldn't even land a sloppy one. My sword felt absurdly heavy. It was a beautiful weapon, finer than anything I'd ever seen in my mercenary days, but even the best blade in Calyari would have felt like a lead weight after hours of incessant training under the worst instructor I'd ever had.

In my own opinion, I deserved a rest. Two weeks ago, I'd helped Lord Raima win one of the fiercest battles of the war. It had been a costly victory, but a victory nonetheless. Of course, the fiend didn't see it that way.

I glared at my master. Although he wasn't planning on sparring with me, he was dressed in a form-fitting black doublet and tall boots, which made him look more like a rogue swordsman than the powerful Deathwalker that he was. He had his feet propped up on a pile of rags which was actually the body of a man he'd killed a few hours ago. The man's chest wasn't moving up and down, but I could tell that the poor bastard was still bleeding out. His blood dribbled through the cracks of the floor in an unnatural way, as if it were trying to run away from Lord Raima.

The fiend watched me with his expressionless black eyes. He sipped on something that I did not think was wine, and his lips left a frosted mark on the rim of his goblet.

"Again," Lord Raima ordered. He rapped his silver staff hard on the floor. A mangled-looking khuri lying on his feet picked its head up and growled. The dog-fiend looked at me and licked its chops.

"Don't even think about it," I warned the khuri.

"If you kill it, I'll need a new one," Lord Raima reminded me.

"You're not making me into one of those things," I said, mostly for my own benefit. I knew I didn't have any real power against the fiend, but I always reminded myself that he'd spared me *because* of my bad attitude.

"Mercy, if you are not useful to me as you are, I *will* make you so. Again!" He barked.

I glared at him. "I've done it a thousand times already!" I protested.

"I know," he replied. "But you have not yet done it *right*."

There was no sense in protesting. Since our last battle, the fiend had only come down from his tower twice, and both times it had been to kill someone. Although I doubted he intended to make me into a khuri, antagonizing him too much was still not a smart move.

I wiped my face on a towel. It smelled like death, and I was sure that I didn't want to know what it had last been used for. I'd been wearing my armor for hours, and my gambeson was completely soaked with sweat. I could feel the steel of my breastplate digging into my shoulders, and underneath my gauntlets, I knew my palms were blistered. I took a deep breath and settled into my guard.

Lord Raima smiled slightly. He spoke an incoherent word, and the baggorth lunged at me. My blade caught the stitches across its throat, and the fiend's head rolled across the floor.

Before I had a chance to recover, Lord Raima gave another command... and his khuri jumped on my back. I cursed and struggled to tear the thing off, feeling its cold teeth snapping at my neck. Tendrils of shadow seized my limbs, and for a moment I thought that the fiend was about to tear my head off. More than once, he'd promised to trap my soul inside one of his monstrous dogs.

"Let me make this perfectly clear, Mercy," Lord Raima said. "You may have done well at Ilshandir. But that does *not* mean you are irreplaceable!"

"I'm not a dog!" I said. "If all you want is another dog, why don't you just kill me?"

"Continue to test me, and I will!" he replied. The khuri growled, its teeth only a few inches from my left ear. The stench of it caused me to grit my teeth.

"I'm trying to teach you something, you fool!" the fiend paused. "You're strong, yes. That's why you've survived as long as you have. But you *are* a dog! You fight like an animal! You must learn to *fight like a man*! Do that, and you will be *unstoppable*."

That complement caught me offguard. Lord Raima never said anything nice to anyone.

Lord Raima sighed heavily. "Maybe you are a lost cause."

The way he said that gave me a whole lot of motivation to do something. Gritting my teeth, I reached out and grabbed the khuri by its silver collar. It snapped at me, and I cracked it across the face with my armored forearm. The fiend yelped and skittered away.

That was when the doors to the room blew open. Lord Raima's daughter, Aerope was standing out in the hall with her hands on her hips. Her eyes darted from her father on his throne to the khuri, which was curled up in the corner, still whimpering from the blow I'd given it. Its bloody pawprints were all over me.

"Father!" Aerope scolded. "What are you doing?"

"I wasn't going to kill him!" the fiend snorted. He snapped his fingers, and the khuri returned to his side. It growled at me.

Aerope helped me to my feet. Her hands were as cold as the khuri's breath.

"Jack is not one of your fiends, Father! He's your very best soldier, and you shouldn't abuse him the way you do!" Aerope sighed.

Lord Raima looked subdued. If the fiend had one weakness, it was his daughter.

"Get out," he ordered gruffly.

"Thank you," I said to Aerope.

I was a bit surprised that she'd defended me, at least until our eyes met. Her eyes were nearly black, but they still carried a faint flicker of amber in them that made her seem almost human. There were no women with the fiend's army, apart from a few old whores. Still, no man dared to set his eyes on Lord Raima's daughter.

Aerope was beautiful, the kind of woman who could have her pick of men. Her long black hair was elaborately braided and piled up on her head. She was dressed in dark purple silk, and her eyes were dramatically lined with kohl. Silver bracelets on her wrists and strands of slate-colored pearls wound around her neck made her look like the princess she was. Aerope always took great pains with her appearance. I wasn't sure who she was trying to impress, but she was becoming very difficult for me to ignore.

Still, I'd seen her fight from a distance during the Battle of Ilshandir. I knew she was a Deathwalker like her father, and as deadly as a sand viper.

"One hour," she whispered in my ear. "Meet me in the library."

The saga continues in the next Paladin book!

Sarah Bellian is a museum curator and historian. She began writing stories in the first grade for her younger siblings. Determined never to grow up, she spends her time fencing and shooting archery with the Society for Creative Anachronism, playing roller derby, and finding interesting places to explore.

Middleman Publishing is a small (very small) publishing company based out of Dayton, Texas. Find us on Facebook and feel free to contact us to learn more about this book series and more at:

middlemanprint@gmail.com